HER BODYGUARD

BODYGUARD SERIES BOOK 1

EMILY HAYES

1

GRAY

"It's a bad idea."

"It'll be fine. A fun night out with my friends is just what I need to forget about this whole Brandon business."

Grayson Reilly ground her teeth as she fought not to glare at Tiffany, reminding herself that Tiffany was a client. "You shouldn't be trying to *forget* about it. Brandon is dangerous. That's why your mother hired me to protect you in the first place. A stalker is nothing to joke about, especially one who leaves dead puppies at your doorstep. He's clearly not afraid of violence."

"Well, that's what you're here for, isn't it? To protect me. You can do it just as well at the club as you can here at home."

"No, I can't." Gray couldn't believe she had to explain this. "Since I started working for you, I've had state-of-the-art security systems installed in and around your home. It would be foolish of Brandon to try to do anything to you here. A club, however, is a different story."

Tiffany shrugged. "It's just one night out. We'll sneak out the back way. Brandon won't even know I'm gone."

Gray knew it wouldn't be that simple. Brandon was smart and kept a careful watch on Tiffany. However, she had already explained all this to Tiffany. The last thing she needed was Tiffany deciding that she was a party pooper and that she needed to be left behind.

Gray resisted the urge to roll her eyes. "Fine, but you're staying close to me at all times."

"Okie dokie," Tiffany agreed easily.

Gray was never working for a spoiled rich brat again. This entire job had been a nightmare. All she wanted was to catch Brandon and hand him over to the police so that she could be done trying to talk sense into Tiffany day in and day out.

Tiffany's friends—equally rich and air-headed —arrived in a limo with a driver. Tiffany was wearing the bare minimum of clothing legally required to stop her from getting arrested for indecent exposure. She grimaced as she looked at Gray. "Are you seriously going clubbing wearing that?"

Gray was wearing her standard work clothes—practical pants, flat leather boots and a top with open sleeves that allowed her freedom of movement, should it come to hand-to-hand combat. "Yes, I'm wearing this."

"They won't allow you in."

"I'm sure you can convince them." Tiffany handed out bribes like candy to get what she wanted.

Tiffany pouted. "I suppose. Still, I think you'd look hot in a dress."

"I'm not trying to look hot," Gray explained patiently. "I'm trying to protect you... and anyway, dresses have never been my thing."

"Fine. Let's go, then."

Gray didn't pay much attention to Tiffany's conversation with her friends on the drive to the club. It was something to do with shopping, something Gray had no interest in. She thought longingly of her time in the army, when she didn't have to deal with any of this nonsense.

Of course, thoughts of her time in the army inevitably brought back thoughts of Amelia.

It had been seven years since Gray had lost her girlfriend to a landmine in Afghanistan, and she'd never really let her go. She'd left the military with a couple of shiny medals for her trouble and a broken heart. Everything had just reminded her too much of Amelia. She couldn't stay.

Starting up her own bodyguarding business had been a natural step. For the most part, Gray liked her job. She'd always found satisfaction in protecting people; it was why she'd joined the army in the first place.

Some clients just ground on her last nerve, and Tiffany was one of those.

They got to the club, and Tiffany did have to hand out a bribe to get Gray in, but other than that, the whole process went smoothly. Tiffany and her friends immediately headed for the dance floor.

As much as Gray would like to stay back and watch, it was too risky. Clubs weren't her scene at all, but she couldn't allow herself to be separated from Tiffany. So, she reluctantly followed them onto the dance floor.

Gray felt extremely self-conscious in amongst all the dancers, trying to blend in. Tiffany was laughing and twirling to the music, having the time of her life with not a care in the world.

Gray, on the other hand, was trying to dance while keeping an eye out in every direction, looking for any sign of Brandon. It was difficult, given how closely everyone was packed together. She didn't like this at all. Brandon could get close to Tiffany under the cover of the crowd and snatch her before Gray had a chance to do anything.

She moved closer to Tiffany, allowing Tiffany to press her back up against Gray's stomach as they danced together. Gray knew that Tiffany was straight, and while she was gay, she felt nothing even with Tiffany's lithe body pressed against her. Gray hadn't felt anything for anyone in a long time, not since Amelia had died.

Tiffany made to pull away, but Gray wrapped an arm around her waist, encouraging Tiffany to keep dancing with her. Tiffany shrugged and continued to wriggle around to the music. Gray hated this, but it had to be done.

It was probably only because she was so close to Tiffany that it happened the way it did.

A squeak was what alerted her.

Her eyes flashed to Lily, one of Tiffany's friends. Gray only looked at Lily for a second, because her attention was immediately caught by the man behind her. His face was only half visible in the shadows of the flashing club lights, but she recognized him at once. Brandon.

He was holding something to Lily's back, no doubt a weapon, which was probably why Lily meekly went with him, off the dance floor and toward the club's back entrance.

Gray hesitated, torn. She knew why Brandon was taking Lily; it was to get Gray to follow. He knew Gray couldn't resist saving an innocent, and once she was safely away from Tiffany, Brandon would circle back and grab his real target.

There was only one thing to do. She had to bring Tiffany with her. Gray hated dragging Tiffany into a dangerous situation, but it was better than leaving her here and waiting for the dangerous situation to come to her.

"Where are we going?" Tiffany hadn't even noticed her friend's disappearance.

"Just come with me."

Tiffany huffed but allowed Gray to pull her by the hand toward the club exit.

There Brandon, holding a gun to Lily's head. Tiffany shrieked and ducked behind Gray.

"It's over, Tiffany. You can't deny our love

forever. Just come to me, my love, and I will let your friend go."

"You're crazy! Go fuck yourself!"

Gray did her best not to wince. It would have been better if Tiffany had at least tried to play along, but she supposed that Tiffany wasn't trained in how best to handle these kinds of situations, so she couldn't really expect her to react like Gray would.

Everything seemed to happen in slow motion. Gray saw Brandon move the gun from Lily's head to point at Tiffany. His finger tightened on the trigger.

She launched herself at him, grabbing his gun hand. It went off with a deafening bang and she felt a blinding pain in her shoulder, but she couldn't think about that right now. She focused all her attention on wrestling the gun from Brandon's grip.

Gray kept in shape, going to the gym and doing strength regularly. Brandon was no match for her. Gray tossed the gun aside and lifted a leg over his torso, so that she was straddling him, turning him onto his stomach. She twisted one of his arms behind his back.

"Stop struggling. Stop." She pulled the arm,

causing Brandon to cry out in pain. "I'll ease up when you relax and stop trying to escape."

"Fuck you!" Brandon kept trying to break free, but Gray simply increased the pressure on his arm until the pain forced him to obey her instruction. He went limp beneath her, panting, and Gray loosened her grip on his arm enough to stop hurting him, but not enough for him to break free.

"Tiffany, please call the police," she said calmly.

Tiffany was hysterical, crying and hyperventilating as she said something completely unintelligible. Gray couldn't get up to comfort her without letting go of Brandon, so she did the best she could from her current position.

"You're alright, Tiffany," she soothed. "It's over. We've got Brandon. Now, we just need to call the police to pick him up. Please, call 911."

Tiffany finally got out her phone and made the call. She wasn't especially coherent, but Gray knew that the operator would trace her location and send officers, as well as paramedics. She became aware of the throbbing in her shoulder. Gray couldn't tell if the bullet was still in there or not, but either way, it was hurting more by the moment.

She adjusted her grip so that she was holding Brandon with her good arm, hoping that she wouldn't pass out from blood loss before the police got there.

Fortunately, the bullet didn't seem to have hit anything important, and she was still very much conscious when the police and paramedics arrived. Gray made sure that Brandon was in cuffs before allowing the paramedics to load her into the ambulance.

She gratefully took the painkiller they offered her and lay back, allowing them to do their thing. Gray had been shot before and she knew it was best just to let the professionals take care of things without interfering.

It turned out that the bullet was still lodged in her shoulder, which meant Gray would need surgery to remove it. Fortunately, her successful business afforded her the best health insurance money could buy, which certainly came in handy in her line of work.

When she woke, it was to a fruit basket and a check with a substantial bonus for saving Tiffany's life. Gray grinned when she saw the check. With this much money, she'd be able to hire a secretary, something she dearly needed now that her business was growing.

She had three retired veterans on her payroll, and managing them and their clients while taking on clients of her own was getting to be a bit much.

She winced as she moved and tugged at the wound in her shoulder. Her arm was in a sling, but it still hurt. Oh well. She'd been hurt worse than this before. Gray supposed she was due for some time off anyway.

Guarding Tiffany had taken a lot of patience, and she needed time to recharge before taking on another client.

She just hoped that her next client was nothing like Tiffany.

Gray swung her arm, gently at first but then with increasing vigor, pleased when it didn't twinge at all. It had taken a couple of months and some careful rehab in the gym, but the doctors had finally cleared her for full duty again. Luckily no lasting damage had been done.

She logged onto her website and listed herself as available as a personal bodyguard again. Next, she checked in with her people, making sure that their jobs were all going well and they had everything they needed.

Gray was just about to make lunch when her phone rang. "Hello, Gray speaking."

"Hi, Grayson Reilly?"

"That's right." No one called her by her full name. This must be important.

"My name is Rochelle. I work for Simon Casey."

The name rang a bell, but Gray couldn't quite place it. "How can I help you, Rochelle?"

"Mr. Casey has instructed me to acquire your services in protecting his daughter, Savannah."

A new client already? Excellent. "I'd be happy to assist you in your application. Is Savannah under any particular threat?"

"I'm afraid I'm not at liberty to discuss that. I'm simply to acquire your services."

"I'd be better able to protect her if I know what I'm up against," Gray pressed.

"You'll have to take that up with Mr. Casey. I'm just the messenger here."

"Fair enough. Do you know how long Savannah will need someone protecting her for?"

"That is also to be determined."

Gray opened her laptop and idly googled Savannah Casey. A quick scan of the results showed her to be very similar to Tiffany—a spoiled rich brat who was only interested in throwing money around. No way was Gray taking on another of those.

Savannah was strikingly beautiful, sharp blue eyes and long golden hair, but beauty wasn't going to sway Gray's decision.

"Well, one of my people should be finishing up with her job in the next few days. I'm sure she'll be happy to assist Savannah."

"No. Mr. Casey instructed me to get you specifically. He's done his research and has heard very good things about you, like how you saved your last client's life."

"I assure you, everyone in my company is exceptionally well-trained and perfectly capable of protecting their clients."

"I'm sorry, but Mr. Casey said it *has* to be Grayson Reilly."

"I'm afraid I'm not available right now."

Gray wondered if Rochelle would call her on her lie, given that she'd just listed herself as available on her website, but Rochelle's response caught her by surprise. "Mr. Casey is prepared to offer you double your usual rate."

Was she hearing correctly? "Double?"

"That's right, as well as a substantial signing bonus."

For that much money, Gray decided that she

would protect anyone, no matter how trying they proved to be.

"Fine, I'll do it. I'll need to meet with Mr. Casey, though. I'll need more details than you seem able to give me."

"Of course. I'll set it up. Thank you, Ms. Reilly."

"Please, call me Gray."

"I'll be seeing you soon, Gray."

The threat to Savannah must be quite urgent, because Mr. Casey reached out to set up a meeting a mere half an hour later, asking to meet before day's end.

Gray got dressed into her more formal clothes that she used to meet with new clients, a black pantsuit and smart boots and drove through town to Mr. Casey's office building. Her dark hair was immaculately smoothed back and tied neatly.

Ah, that's why the name had sounded familiar. She looked up at the huge building with *Casey Enterprises* written in big letters across the top. She didn't know exactly what they did, but she thought she remembered that it was something to do with imports and exports.

Rochelle escorted her up to Mr. Casey's office, where he was waiting for her. "Ms. Reilly, please come in."

"Mr. Casey, Grayson Reilly."

"Simon." He shook her hand firmly and gestured for her to sit down opposite his desk. "Well, Rochelle said you have some questions about the job."

"That's right. I need to know if there is any specific threat to Savannah's life that has prompted you to get her a bodyguard."

"I'm afraid there is. In the business world, one can't help but make enemies. I seem to have picked up a few. I've gotten some phone calls and emails saying that if I don't cooperate, Savannah will be killed or hurt."

Gray nodded, getting out a small note pad and jotting a few points down. "What, exactly, are their demands?"

"I'm afraid I can't discuss that."

Gray raised an eyebrow. "Simon, you just revealed that your daughter's life is under threat. What could possibly be more important than protecting her?"

"Unfortunately, some things simply need to remain confidential."

"I have no interest in stealing your business secrets, if that's what you're concerned about. I've got my own business to worry about. I can assure you that I have no intention to cause any trouble for yours."

"I believe you, Ms. Reilly. Please don't think that I'm holding back because I think you're going to double-cross me. I've done my research and I know you're the real thing; I wouldn't be entrusting Savannah's life to you if you weren't. There are simply some things I can't discuss."

This was weird. Usually, when a client's life was under threat, they were more than willing to disclose every aspect of the threat. It was necessary for Gray to be able to do her job. What was Simon involved in that he refused to talk to her, even when his daughter's life was on the line?

Well, whatever it was, Gray was going to find out. She didn't make a habit of walking into a job unprepared, and she wasn't about to start now. She had contacts, both from her work and her time in the military. She would get to the bottom of this, whether Simon wanted her to or not.

For now, she needed to pretend to cooperate with his ridiculous wish that she walk into the job blind. "I understand. Is there anything else you can tell me?"

"Savannah is independent. She likes to do her own thing and doesn't like being told what to do. I don't think she'll take well to the idea that I've hired her a bodyguard."

Just great. She was sounding more and more like Tiffany by the moment.

"Understood. I hope she will come around."

Simon didn't look convinced, but he nodded. "When are you available to start?"

She'd need some time to look into the threat to Savannah, but if the threat was as real as Simon seemed to think it was, Gray couldn't afford to take too much time. "I can start on Monday, if that works for you."

"Monday is perfect. Thank you, Ms. Reilly. Please see Rochelle on your way out. She will sort out payment details with you. You will be very well compensated for your work."

The signing bonus was indeed substantial— definitely worth the time Gray would need to put into figuring out what in the world was going on here. She spent the rest of the afternoon making phone calls, sending emails and doing research.

It seemed that Casey Enterprises was a global shipping company that offered the most competitive rates on the market. At first glance, everything looked aboveboard, but not long after she had sat down to do her own research, Gray got a call from Jason.

Jason was a computer genius who had done some contract work with her unit in Afghanistan and could figure out anyone's secrets given a laptop and an internet connection.

"Hey, Jason. That was quick."

"Well, it didn't take much time to figure out that the business you asked me to investigate is shady as hell. You know those competitive shipping rates they offer? They are only able to offer those because they have a huge smuggling operation going, allowing them to avoid import taxes."

That would explain why Simon had been so reluctant to talk to her. "If it's such a big operation, why hasn't the government caught on?"

"Oh, they have, but they haven't been able to pin anything on Casey. He's very smart and covers his tracks well. They're trying, but so far they haven't had any luck. Even what I have is only circumstantial and would never hold up in court."

"So, do you have any idea who's threatening to kill the girl?"

"It could be any number of people, but my best bet is Herom Couriers."

"Why them?"

"They're Casey Enterprises' biggest competitor, and they're losing a lot of money because of the shortcuts Casey is taking. They can't afford to keep up with his rates, given that they haven't figured out how to dodge taxes the way he has—not that they wouldn't do it if they could, given what I've read about them. I can totally see them threatening his daughter to try to get him to share his secrets."

"Thanks, Jason. I owe you one."

"No problem. It sounds like you have your work cut out for you on this one."

"Yeah, I do. I'll figure it out, though. I always do."

"Well, good luck."

"Thanks. I'll need it."

They hung up, leaving Gray in thoughtful silence. From what research she had done of Savannah, she seemed to have distanced herself from the rest of the family, withdrawing to a mansion on the opposite side of the city and having minimal contact with them.

Did she know about her father's shady business dealings? Was that why she wanted to put space between him and her, or was she simply young and acting out? Gray knew from her research that Savannah had chosen to be a model rather than join her father's business. Was it just a phase, or did she truly want out of that world?

Gray's conscience squirmed at the thought of working for Simon knowing what she knew about him. Should she not be going to the police with her information? No, Jason had said that it was all circumstantial. Going to the police would accomplish nothing except Gray losing this job, which meant she wouldn't be able to protect Savannah.

Gray may not like spoiled rich girls, but that didn't mean she wanted Savannah to die, and she knew that there were few people as well equipped to protect her as she was. And she couldn't get Savannah's dazzling blue eyes out of her head.

She didn't know how long she'd need to protect Savannah for, but Gray had learned the hard way that passive protection to an active threat only went so far. If she truly wanted to protect her client, she needed to take steps to find the person who wanted to hurt them and bring them to justice.

If she could capture one of the people Herom had hired to go for Savannah and hand him in to the police, Herom would surely go down. Criminals for hire had no loyalty and would not hesitate to take the deal the police would offer them in exchange for their information. With whoever was threatening Savannah behind bars, the threat to her would be removed, and Gray could move on to other cases.

Gray had never failed to protect a client short term or long term, and she didn't intend to start now. Savannah may not be happy about getting a bodyguard, but she would become more appreciative when bullets started flying; they all did.

Gray was still waiting to hear from some more of her contacts, hoping to hear more details about Simon's shady business dealings. While she was waiting, she started looking into Herom Couriers and began reaching feelers out to her people to try to gather information on them.

From what she could discover, Herom was mostly aboveboard, and their CEO was decent. However, the new manager, who was just under the CEO in the corporate ladder, was ruthless. It seemed that he would do anything to get promoted to the top job, even threaten innocent women in order to obtain lower shipping costs.

That's the one Gray would need to go after. She toyed with the idea of calling up the CEO and telling him the truth about what was going on but discarded the idea. It wouldn't be that simple. Erik had gotten into the position he had because Richard trusted him, and Richard wasn't going to take a stranger's word over his top manager's.

No, she'd need to do this the hard way. If Jason had it right, sooner or later, Erik would hire someone to go after Savannah, and then Gray would have her chance.

She just hoped that Savannah didn't make her job too nightmarish along the way.

3

SAVANNAH

"Nice big smile. There's a good girl."

Savannah resisted the urge to make a face. She wasn't anyone's good girl, but she kept her smile firmly in place as she looked into the camera. It clicked away for a few moments before the director called it.

"Alright, cut. Good work, Savannah. We'll need you again after the next shoot, in the bathing suit this time."

"Sure thing."

Savannah hated the waiting around between shoots, but it was an inevitable part of being a model. She went over to chat with some of the other models while she waited. There was a new brand of designer handbags coming out next month and they were discussing their various pre-orders.

Savannah had ordered the pink and gold one over a week ago. She was planning to go out with her friends to show it off as soon as it arrived.

The other models were nice enough, but Savannah didn't miss the jealous glances they threw her way. She knew that most of them would do anything to be her. She had everything a girl could ever want—money, beauty, a long line of women desperate to date her. Fame had never interested her in the way it interested some of the others.

She didn't want to be recognizable on the street. The last thing she needed was reporters following her everywhere. No, she was happy to be just another airbrushed face on the pages of a fashion magazine.

She thought wistfully of her painting supplies back home. She wouldn't get any time to paint today as this shoot was bound to finish late.

Savannah had been dodging calls from her agent recently. She had moved to her mansion out of town supposedly to be alone and focus on her modeling career, but really, she had just wanted some peace. She loved painting, but it was hardly what was expected of someone of her social standing.

It wasn't that she didn't enjoy the perks of her station—the shopping, the easy sex, the parties—it was all great. She just wished that people would accept her following her passion as well as doing the typical rich girl things.

However, every time she had mentioned painting to anyone, they had looked at her as though she were crazy, so Savannah had learned to keep her passion to herself. At first, she had loved the modeling, but her enthusiasm for it had waned over the years, and now, she only did one shoot every couple of months to satisfy her agent.

The shoot before her next one took longer than they had anticipated, and it was evening by the time Savannah was called up to do her final shoot. Her body was aching from the poses and she felt like she was selling out as she leant forward as requested to give a good view of her cleavage.

Savannah knew her body was as striking as her face and understood that photographers wanted to photograph it. But the further she went with the modelling, the more she thought, it just wasn't for her. It all felt so empty. So objectifying.

The shoot finally finished, and she headed home. She listened to voice notes from various friends and acquaintances from the back of the car as her driver took her home. There were two party invitations and a request for a shopping buddy. Savannah had responded in the affirmative to all of them by the time the car came to a halt.

She was just about to get into the shower when her phone rang. She looked at in surprise when she saw who was calling.

"Hi, Dad." She hadn't had much contact with her father since their last fight, when he had tried to get her to move back home. Something about a threat to her life by a business rival. Like Savannah was interested in his boring business stuff. No one had tried to kill her yet.

"Savannah, how are you?"

"I'm fine, thank you, and you?"

She waited impatiently while they exchanged pleasantries. Finally, Simon got down to what he had called about.

"I know you're not willing to move home, despite the threat to your life, so I've found another solution. I've hired you a bodyguard."

"You've done what?"

"Her name is Grayson Reilly, and she'll be starting on Monday."

"What the fuck, Dad?! You can't just hire someone to follow me around without asking my permission!"

"Well, I figured you'd react this way, so—"

"Damn right I'm reacting this way! You have no right to go behind my back on this. If this woman starts following me around, I'm going to report her to the police for stalking, because that's what it will be if I don't consent to her presence."

"Don't be like that, Savannah." Simon's voice became low and dangerous. "I would hate to have to pull your access to your trust fund, but I will if I need to. If that's the only way to keep you safe—to force you to move home by freezing your funds— then I will do it. I'm not risking your life. This is not optional."

Savannah ground her teeth, biting back the urge to fling obscenities at her father. This wasn't the first time he'd used money to threaten her, and she hated him for it. She didn't make nearly enough from her modelling to fund her lifestyle, she was reliant on his money and she hated it. "Fine," she bit out. "I won't report her to the police, and I'll let her in the house, but that's all I'm promising."

"That's all I ask. Thank you, Savannah."

As if she'd had any choice. "Bye."

She hung up, still fuming. Savannah paced up and down her room, trying to work off her agitation. How dare he? She was a grown woman, and he had no right to interfere with her life like this. It was her life, and she would decide if it was under threat, thank you very much.

Of course, as long as he had power over her, Simon could do what he wanted. He had thrown a fit and threatened to disown her when Savannah had tried to put the money she earned from modeling into a separate account in her name, insisting instead that it go to her trust, which he controlled, thus maintaining his control over her.

She had even considered getting another job on the side, something he didn't know about, which would allow her to put funds away without him knowing, but she had never studied and didn't have any marketable skills. Being able to shop for nine hours straight was hardly going to land her a job.

Well, Savannah wasn't going to play his game. She would do what she said she would; she would allow this Grayson Reilly in the house, but she'd never said anything about cooperating. She was certain she could make the bodyguard quit within a week.

Savannah grabbed her phone, scrolling through various messages. She needed to unwind, and the best way to do that was in bed with a beautiful woman. She quickly selected someone and sent out a text.

Unsurprisingly, she got a quick affirmative response. Savannah showered while she waited for Megan to arrive and got dressed into just a silk robe with some minimal makeup. This would be just what she needed to forget all about this bodyguard nonsense.

Monday arrived too soon for Savannah's liking. She was determined to get on with her life as usual while being as hostile as possible in an effort to get this new bodyguard to leave. If she was lucky, this Grayson Reilly would be gone by the end of the day. If she was unlucky, the end of the week for sure.

Savannah was lounging on the couch in her

favorite black lace underwear, determined to make the new bodyguard uncomfortable, when she heard a new voice conversing with her maid on her way in the front door. The voice was deep and husky and really quite sexy.

Savannah looked over as the owner of the voice entered the room after the maid. The woman was tall and masculine in appearance with dark hair slicked back. She wore black jeans and a black shirt, her muscular arms popping under the short sleeves of the shirt. The brown leather belt she wore looked well worn and effortlessly casual. Her eyes darted around the room taking in her surroundings. Savannah couldn't pin the color of them from this distance- were they grey? They were intense, that was for sure.

This was the sexiest woman Savannah had ever seen.

She watched the woman's eyes widen slightly and then return to normal quickly as though not to give anything away as her glance took in Savannah's body in the underwear before quickly returning to her face.

Savannah was sure she could see hunger in her eyes.

"You must be Savannah. It's nice to meet you. I'm Gray."

"What kind of name is Gray, anyway?" Savannah didn't look at Gray or get up to take her proffered hand. She leant back on the couch, knowing that her beautiful body was on full display.

Gray didn't seem phased.

"It's actually Grayson, but I prefer Gray. I was named after my grandfather."

Savannah shrugged and went back to watching the fashion show on TV.

"Right. I'll just get myself settled in, then."

Gray followed Hannah the maid, who was, unfortunately, her usual, helpful self, despite Savannah's instructions to the contrary. Hannah didn't have a mean bone in her body and probably couldn't bring herself to be rude to Gray, no matter how much Savannah insisted to ensure that Gray felt unwelcome.

Savannah couldn't help herself as she sneakily glanced at Gray's muscular arms.

Fuck, that woman is so damn sexy!

She sighed. Hannah was good at what she did. Savannah certainly wasn't going to do the cleaning and cooking herself, and she trusted Hannah, which was important when you were going to have someone in your house for most of the day every day.

Savannah turned her attention back to the TV screen. She pointedly ignored Gray when Gray came to stand behind her. Surely, Gray would get bored sooner or later.

It seemed that Gray didn't bore easily, even when Savannah switched the channel to a sitcom so dull that it almost had her falling asleep. At least Gray had the sense not to try to make conversation with her.

Savannah snuck a look at Gray out of the corner of her eye. Gray was standing in a relaxed pose with her feet shoulder spread and her hands clasped behind her back. Her intense eyes were constantly moving, flicking from Savannah to the doors and the windows in the room.

Surely she would get tired of standing eventually? Savannah didn't offer Gray a seat, and Gray didn't ask for one. As the afternoon wore on, Savannah became increasingly frustrated. Gray just was not taking the hint. Maybe she'd have to be more obvious.

"I don't know why my father even bothered to hire someone so *old* to guard me," Savannah sneered. "I bet you couldn't win a fight against a child."

It was a blatant lie. Gray was older than Savannah, but she couldn't be much past forty. Quite apart from that, there were the goddamn popping muscles that Savannah couldn't stop herself from looking at. This bodyguard was clearly in superb shape. She had a gun strapped onto her hip and Savannah thought she could see a knife in her boot. There was such an aura of toughness around her.

If Savannah really had feared for her life, she would have felt comforted to have someone like Gray protecting her.

But she was sure that this was just another play by her father to keep her under his control. He was paying Gray, after all. She was probably a spy, to ensure that Savannah didn't try to put any more money away somewhere Simon couldn't control it.

"I suppose we'll have to see," Gray said in an infuriatingly calm voice.

"No, we won't *see*. You're just an ornament here. Are you seriously too dumb to realize that? My father just wants to keep tabs on me. The next time he hands over your paycheck, he'll be wanting a full report on my activities."

"I wouldn't do that to you, Savannah. Your father may be paying me, but you are my client, and I would never abuse your trust. Whatever happens while I am guarding you is private, even from your father."

"He'll fire you if you don't cooperate."

Gray shrugged. "If that's the case, then I guess you don't need protecting after all, and I'll simply move on to other clients. I'm not compromising my morals for money. I have never ever broken a client's privacy and I don't intend to start now."

Savannah's instinct was to disbelieve her. Everyone lied. Everyone. But Gray seemed so sincere, it was difficult to convince herself that Gray was being dishonest.

"Right. Well, if you're going to be here, you may as well do something useful. Go mop the floor or something. Don't just stand there."

"I'm afraid I'm unable to help you in that regard. I need to be alert and watching for potential threats. I can't do that if I'm focused on housework. Would you like me to call Hannah?"

Savannah had been hoping Gray would take offense at the suggestion, but Gray seemed infuriatingly unflappable.

"No, it's fine," Savannah snapped. "Hannah knows when she's wanted and when she isn't."

Gray didn't respond. Savannah ground her teeth and stared unseeingly at the TV screen. There had to be something she could do to put Gray off. She would have to think of something. No way was she putting up with this irritatingly competent woman's presence long term.

Savannah spent the rest of the day watching TV, hoping to bore Gray, or at least tire her out, but Gray never asked to sit down, or even shifted her weight around like she was uncomfortable. Was she some sort of standing champion? Statue of the year?

Savannah sat down for dinner that evening and grudgingly offered Gray a plate of food. She may be pissed, but she wasn't going to let a guest starve under her roof, no matter how unwelcome that guest was. And sexy...

Stop it, Savannah.

"Thank you," Gray murmured, taking the plate without another word. Even as she ate, her eyes never stopped moving, as if there were threats to Savannah's life lurking in every shadow. It was making Savannah jumpy, like there really was something to fear. She rolled her eyes. This was just another power play by her father, nothing more.

"We need to talk about your security."

Savannah made a face. "Isn't that what you're here for?"

"Yes, but I can't be everywhere at once, and even I need to sleep. I want to install cameras all around the house, as well as electric fences, double locks on all the doors and bars on the windows."

"Are you insane? I'm not going to be a prisoner in my own house."

"You wouldn't be a prisoner. You'd be free to come and go as you wish. The security measures are to keep intruders out, not to keep you in."

"I know that!" Savannah snapped. "I'm not stupid, you know." Just because she was a model who liked to throw money around didn't mean she was a brainless twit like some of the women in the industry.

"Then I'm sure you see the necessity of these measures."

Savannah scowled at Gray. "No, I don't. I've told you, I'm not in any real danger."

"If that's true, then it means we'll have made your place more secure and safer for no reason. However, if you're wrong, you'll be dead. I'm sure you can see why I'm in favor of the former option."

Savannah could see Gray's point, but she wasn't going to admit it. "Whatever." She wasn't going to put up with this shit. Maybe her father thought that if he made life miserable enough for her, she would agree to move back home. Well, he had another thing coming. She would drive Gray and her stupid security measures out, and her life would go back to normal.

They finished the rest of their dinner in frosty silence.

Savannah showered, making a point of prancing across the hall in front of Gray dressed in nothing but a towel. She didn't miss how Gray's eyes followed her briefly before Gray wrenched them away. Savannah felt a rush of desire through her body.

Ugh, why is this woman so sexy?

It wasn't surprising that Gray was attracted to her. Anyone who had any interest in women was attracted to her. Savannah wondered if she could use this to help her get rid of Gray once and for all. However, would it be harder for Savannah, given that for once, the attraction was reciprocated.

She scrolled through her phone, checking

messages and looking at pictures. She picked out Rose, one of the models she had worked with a couple of times. Yes, Rose would do nicely.

Savannah sent Rose a message inviting her over the next day.

Oh, this was going to be fun.

The next morning, Savannah completely ignored Gray through breakfast, and Gray was smart enough not to try to make conversation. The doorbell rang just as Savannah was finishing her toast. Hannah got it, and a minute later, three men with armfuls of equipment trooped into the house.

"Um, who are you?"

"We're here to install your new security measures, Miss."

"I didn't order any security measures."

"I did." Gray looked completely unabashed as Savannah glared at her. "Your father was kind enough to pay for the necessary upgrades to your security, and I arranged for them to happen as soon as possible. The sooner we get your place secured, the better."

Savannah clenched her hands under the table, silently fuming. She could send the workmen away, but word would no doubt get back to Simon, and she didn't doubt that he would simply threaten her into doing as he commanded again. It was an awful, helpless feeling, not having control over her own life, but there was nothing Savannah could do about it.

She decided that the best she could do was ignore the workmen and get on with her plan to get rid of Gray. Once Gray was gone, she could hire her own workmen to get rid of the stupid bars on her windows and whatever else Gray had ordered, and without Gray looking over her shoulder, there would be no one to report her defiance to her father.

Rose came over an hour later. She and Savannah sipped coffee by the pool before getting into their bikinis. They took a quick dip before going to lie on the deck in the sun.

Gray was still an irritating presence at Savannah's back.

"Does she ever leave?" Rose whispered, casting a glance at Gray.

"Not yet," Savannah muttered. "I'm working on it."

Rose giggled. "She's quite *hot*, isn't she?"

Savannah grimaced. It obviously hadn't escaped her that Gray was indeed very hot. She was so dignified and put-together. She had an aura

of toughness and that effortless masculine look
that Savannah couldn't help but find attractive.
That just made her feel even more resentful of
Gray than ever.

"Not as hot as you." Savannah gave Rose her
most seductive smile and leaned in to kiss her.

Rose returned the kiss eagerly, and soon,
Savannah was forgetting all about Gray as she got
lost in the kiss with Rose. They entwined themselves on the deck, pressing their bodies together,
letting their hands slide under the thin fabric of
each other's bikinis.

Savannah was halfway through taking Rose's
bikini top off when Rose pulled back. "Wait."

Savannah pulled back. "You good?"

"More than good, but remember, we have an
audience."

"Just ignore her." Savannah leaned in for
another kiss, but Rose turned away, and Savannah
pouted.

"Not in front of the help, Savannah! Let's go to
your room."

Savannah gave Rose a sparkling smile. "Whatever you want."

She took Rose by the hand and led her through

the house, glancing back over her shoulder as she did so. Unsurprisingly, Gray followed.

Well, if Rose wasn't comfortable doing it in front of Gray, Savannah would just have to make sure that she was loud enough for Gray to enjoy the show from the other side of the door.

Oh, this was going to be *fun*.

4

GRAY

G ray felt bad watching Savannah. Of course, that was ridiculous. It was her job to watch Savannah, but did Savannah really need to make it so difficult? Gray knew that she was intruding on something private, but she couldn't very well turn her back just because watching Savannah make out with a woman on the deck was making her uncomfortable.

Gray clenched her teeth as another wave of arousal went through her. What was wrong with her? She hadn't had feelings like this for anyone in years, ever since she'd lost Amelia. What was it about this silly rich girl and her obvious beauty that was suddenly awakening desire in her?

It wasn't like Gray hadn't had attractive clients before, nor that she hadn't witnessed them getting hot and heavy with a partner. She was doing a terrible job of looking out for threats right now, because she couldn't tear her eyes from Savannah, and all she could think about was various reasons to excuse herself to the bathroom so that she could get herself off.

Of course, that would be entirely unprofessional and Gray wouldn't do it. That didn't stop her from fantasizing about it, though.

She followed Savannah to her room. Savannah shut the door in Gray's face without a backward glance. Gray sighed. She would have liked to have checked the room first, but no way was she going in there now, where Savannah and Rose were no doubt undressing each other right at this moment.

Savannah moaned loudly, and Gray couldn't help but imagine what Rose might be doing to her. Was she touching Savannah's lovely full breasts? Her clit? Gray wondered what Savannah's breasts looked like exposed. She had already seen more of them than she had expected to, thanks to Savannah prancing around in her underwear, but she had yet to catch a glimpse of Savannah's nipples. What color were they? How big were they?

She forcibly pulled herself out of that line of thinking. She was meant to be thinking about how to protect Savannah's life, not fantasizing about the color of her nipples.

It was difficult, though, especially when she heard deep moans through the door, accompanied by Savannah's enthusiastic cries of pleasure.

There was a banging noise as the headboard of the bed hit the wall repeatedly. Gray was throbbing between her legs and was sorely tempted to slip a hand into her pants to bring herself some relief. It's not like anyone would know. Savannah was certainly too distracted right now to come out and check on Gray.

Gray would know, though. She prided herself on her professionalism, and she wasn't going to give in to this.

"Oh fuck, yes, Rose. Just like that. Yeah. Oh yes, right there. Rose, I'm going to come. Fuck, keep going, please. Rose... ROSE, YES!"

Savannah screamed as she came, and by the sounds of it, Rose wasn't far behind. Gray wondered who was doing what to who. Maybe they were 69ing? The mental image that created was positively tantalizing.

Gray couldn't help but imaging herself with Savannah, fucking her with her favorite strap on. She wished she was packing right now, but that wasn't something she would ever do at work. She moaned softly and leaned back against the wall, positively dizzy with need.

It was no good. She couldn't work like this. Fuck unprofessional. Gray was too distracted to protect herself right now should a threat arise, let alone protect Savannah.

She walked quickly to the nearest bathroom, breaking into a jog for the last few steps, desperate for release. The home was swarming with workmen instaling security measures. It would be a terrible time for a potential threat to choose to attack Savannah. Gray reasoned Savannah was as safe as could be for the next 5 minutes.

She locked the door behind herself and pushed her pants down, bringing her fingers immediately to her clit. Gray moaned softly in relief as she started rubbing herself hard and fast. She remembered Savannah's noises of pleasure and imagined Savannah making those noises under her, in response to Gray's touch.

Gray felt her thighs tightening as pleasure spiraled through her whole body, going outward from her clit.

She clapped her free hand over her mouth as she came hard, her legs nearly giving out with the strength of her release.

Too late, Gray realized that she had squirted all over the bathroom floor. She had miraculously missed her pants, thank God.

She scrambled to get her pants on and mopped the mess up with some toilet paper. She knew that her face must be bright red and was glad that no one was around to see it. What the hell had she just done? She'd gotten off thinking about a client —while she was supposed to be guarding said client, no less.

Gray hurried back to Savannah's room, berating herself the whole way.

When she got back to her post outside Savannah's door, she expected to hear silence, or maybe some pillow talk, but instead, the headboard was banging against the wall once more. They were at it *again*, already?

Fuck, this was going to be a long day.

Several hours later, Rose and Savannah emerged, both freshly showered, appearing satisfied and sated. Gray did her best not to glare at them. She felt the opposite of satisfied or sated. She had point-blank refused to excuse herself to the bathroom again, no matter how turned on she felt, which left her more frustrated than she could remember being in a long time.

Savannah completely ignored Gray as she saw Rose out, giving her a long, wet parting kiss, glancing at Gray just as she pulled away with a knowing glint in her sparkling blue eyes.

The little shit. She was doing this on purpose. She knew how she affected Gray and was deliberately teasing her, probably in an attempt to get Gray to leave.

Well, Savannah wasn't the only one who could be stubborn. Savannah may be a pain in the ass, but that didn't mean Gray wanted her to die. She would do whatever it took to protect her, no matter how difficult Savannah made it.

"I want to go shopping."

Great, just what Gray needed—to inflict herself on the public when she was in such a foul mood already. She didn't see the point in trying to convince Savannah otherwise, though. it would do no good. Savannah was wearing a blue sundress. It was loose fitting and short and her long tan legs drew Gray's eyes. She wasn't wearing a bra and Gray caught glimpses of her nipples.

Focus, Gray!

"Of course. Lead the way."

Gray and Savannah got to the car. Gray sat in the front passenger seat next to the driver so she could see everything and Savannah was in the back where she was safest. Savannah gave the driver instructions to go to the nearest mall.

Gray spent very little time in malls out of choice, preferring to do her shopping online where possible. Savannah, on the other hand, seemed completely at home there. She pranced from shop to shop, waving her credit card around and spending more money than Gray earned in a month.

She handed her parcels to Gray to carry, as though Gray was her servant. Gray wanted to refuse—she had some dignity, after all—but she was well aware that she was on tenuous ground with Savannah as it was. She worried that if she pushed back too much, Savannah would send her away, and then there would be no one to protect her from whoever Herom sent.

So, Gray carried the increasingly ridiculous

load of parcels, eventually calling the driver to collect the bags.

Gray was practically bored to tears and quickly becoming exhausted by the ordeal, but Savannah showed no signs of tiring or getting bored. On the contrary, she seemed to get more and more energized the longer this went on. Where the hell was she getting all of her energy from? Did sex give her some kind of boost, or was she always like this? That blue dress on her that matched her eyes exactly was incredibly distracting.

Eventually, Savannah slowed down just enough for them to eat at a fancy restaurant. Gray was used to eating at posh places with clients. It was a privilege of the job that she never got bored of. Gray recovered slightly having eaten and drank only for them to be thrown back into the shopping nightmare.

Savannah bought everything from clothes to crystal ornaments to fancy hanging mirrors. The clothes were by far the worst.

"Gray, come and take a look at this."

Gray sighed and pulled aside the curtain in the change room. Savannah was dressed in a red miniskirt and a top so tight and low that Gray was surprised her breasts weren't spilling out of it every time she took a breath.

"Well?" Savannah did a twirl, showing off how good her ass looked in that skirt. "What do you think?"

"It's lovely," Gray said in a strangled voice.

"Which between these two?"

Savannah turned her back and took off the top, making Gray's mouth go dry. If Savannah turned around now, Gray would have a full view of her breasts. If that happened, Gray didn't think she'd be able to prevent herself from doing something like kissing her client.

Thankfully, Savannah put the other top on before turning. This one wasn't as tight as the other one, but it was so low cut that Gray was sure she was less than an inch away from seeing Savannah's nipples.

"Well? Which one is better?"

"Um... they're both nice."

Savannah rolled her eyes. "That's not how this works, Gray. You need to pick one."

"Why? You're going to buy both anyway."

"I suppose." Savannah rolled her eyes again. "You're no fun."

She pulled the curtain closed, leaving Gray to

take a long, deep breath, trying to settle herself. So what if Savannah was getting naked just on the other side of that curtain? Gray could be professional. She forcibly shoved the memory of the morning's highly unprofessional masturbation session out of her mind. It had been a once-off slip. That was all. Everyone messed up sometimes, even professionals. She would make sure that it didn't happen again.

Savannah finally finished in the dressing room and came out with an armful of clothes.

"Are we done?" Gray asked hopefully.

"In this shop, yes. There's a new designer store I want to try out."

Gray bit back a groan. "I can't wait."

Savannah kept them at it until the mall closed. Gray couldn't believe that they actually had to be asked to leave by mall security, as they needed to lock up for the night.

Gray had called the driver twice more to take bags to the car. Savannah refused to help carry anything and Gray knew she had to keep her hands free to protect Savannah from any threats.

Savannah flopped into her seat in the car, leaving Gray to help the driver get the last pile of bags into the trunk. There were so many, the driver had to unpack the earlier bags to find the best way to make everything fit. Gray briefly considered just leaving the bags out on the sidewalk and going home without them. It would serve Savannah right for acting so bratty, as Gray was sure that this ridiculously prolonged shopping trip was as much to annoy her as it was to satisfy Savannah's rich girl appetites.

She smothered the nasty impulse and helped pack the bags into the trunk without complaint. The door to the back seat was open and Gray looked in, Savannah was lying across the back seat, her flat pumps were off and her long smooth legs were crossed.

"I could really use a foot rub. Help me out, Gray?"

No fucking way was Gray giving her a foot rub. *Gray* was the one who needed a foot rub. She was used to standing and walking around all day, but today had been exhausting even for her, and her feet were aching. At least Savannah had put herself through all that willingly.

"I'm afraid I can't help you there." She endeavored to keep her voice light and friendly, though she feared it came out more snappish than she intended.

Savannah pouted but didn't argue. She was so cute when she pouted, it almost made Gray change her mind, but the last thing she needed was to blur lines with Savannah even more than she already had. Savannah seemed determined to wash away all boundaries, but that didn't mean Gray was going to cooperate with her.

Gray got in her place in the front of the car.

When they got home, Savannah called her massage therapist, requesting a home visit for an "emergency" foot rub.

Sure enough, half an hour later, a woman carrying a bag of essential oils arrived. It seemed Savannah already had a massage bed set up in one of her many spare rooms. Gray watched enviously as Savannah got her feet pampered.

Did she *have* to moan like that? She sounded so much like she did when she was having sex, if Gray hadn't been watching her, she would have sworn that Savannah was having sex again.

When it ended, Savannah wandered through to the dining room, where dinner was waiting for them. Gray supposed she must have texted her chef to let him know when they would be arriving home.

Gray gratefully tucked in to yet another deli-

cious meal. There were many things she could crit-
icize about her stay here so far, but the food was
beyond reproach.

Finally—finally—Savannah went to bed. Gray
had feared that she would invite someone over for
the night, but it seemed that Savannah had finally
worn herself out.

"Wait. I need to check your room before you go
to sleep."

"There's no one in there."

"You don't know that," Gray explained
patiently. "Even with top-of-the-line security
measures, it's possible for people to sneak through
if they're really determined. It'll only take a
minute."

"Fine." Savannah rolled her eyes and allowed
Gray to go in before her. Gray did a quick search of
the room, and finding it free of any threat, let
Savannah in. Savannah was already undressing
before Gray had even left the room.

As tempted as she was to linger, Gray forced
herself out of the room and closed the door behind
her. She went through to the room where she'd
had the workers set up a watch station for the
security cameras.

She checked the feed, satisfied to see nothing

suspicious. Only once she had gone through everything did Gray finally go to bed. She would shower in the morning. Right now, she was too exhausted by the day to do anything other than go to sleep.

Unfortunately, her sleep was far from restful.

Her traitorous mind served up dreams of Savannah half-naked, smiling seductively at Gray and pulling her closer, kissing her slowly before undressing her and letting Gray fuck her against that headboard so hard that it broke.

Gray woke up sweaty and so turned on it hurt.

She tossed and turned, trying to get back to sleep, but her clit was throbbing and every time she turned over her legs pressed together ever so slightly, giving her a small measure of relief, after which just came more frustration when she didn't follow up with anything more.

It wasn't like Gray was meant to be watching Savannah right now. Maybe it wouldn't be too bad to give in just once more. After all, what she did in her own time, when she wasn't actively watching her client, was up to her. Wasn't it? Gray still felt like this was wrong, but her mind was too muddled with lust to come up with a good counterargument.

With a small whimper of surrender, she

brought her hand to her clit. She was already wet from the dream, and Gray's fingers slipped easily over her clit. She wished she had a toy with her, but she hadn't thought she would need to bring any.

She masturbated, sure, but it had always been a quick thing to bring relief, more of a necessity than a pleasure. With thoughts of Savannah fresh on her mind, Gray found herself wanting to draw this out, to enjoy it.

Savannah probably had plenty of toys, but Gray would rather set herself on fire than go and ask to borrow one.

So, Gray made do with her fingers, trying not to think of Savannah and failing miserably. Her orgasm snuck up on her, coming with unexpected strength. It was all Gray could do not to cry out as she came hard for her own fingers.

Panting, she realized too late that she should have put a towel down. She didn't usually squirt when she was solo, but it seemed that when it came to Savannah, her body was reacting in new and interesting ways, ways Gray didn't like at all.

She crept out of her room, dearly hoping that Savannah was deeply asleep. Gray went to the laundry cupboard and grabbed a spare sheet. She changed the sheet, throwing the one with a wet patch in the wash.

She just hoped that whoever did the washing didn't make a comment to Savannah about the sheet. Surely, they wouldn't. Savannah didn't seem like the type of person to take an interest in laundry.

Now that her body was sated, Gray found that sleep came easily. She drifted off, and this time, her dreams were thankfully free of the temptation that went by the name of Savannah.

5

SAVANNAH

Savannah was frustrated, to say the least. It had been a week, and Gray was *still* following her around like an over-protective German Shepherd. Savanah didn't get it. She'd done everything she possible could to make Gray uncomfortable, and she could tell it was working. Gray was definitely not having a fun time guarding her.

And yet, Gray persisted. Simon must be paying her a lot to put up with all the shit Savannah was throwing at her.

Well, Savannah wasn't going to lose at this game. Gray was stubborn, but so was Savannah, and she didn't like losing. She had a plan.

"I've got a shoot today, Gray."

"Where is it? We should go early so that I can scout the location for any potential threats."

Savannah rolled her eyes, something she had been doing a lot more often of late. "There aren't going to be any threats. It's a modeling shoot, not a war zone."

"I would like to check it anyway."

"Sure, we can go early."

Savannah deliberately dawdled in getting dressed, ignoring Gray's attempts to chivvy her along, so that they arrived mere minutes before the shoot was supposed to start. Gray scowled but didn't say anything as she did a quick check of the perimeter, never straying far from Savannah.

"Who's that?" Amelia, the model Savannah was working with today, cast a glance at Gray, who was watching them with a neutral expression.

"My bodyguard," Savannah muttered resentfully.

"Sounds serious. Are you in danger?"

Savannah sighed. "No, it's just my father making another power play. I'm doing my best to put her off."

Amelia giggled. "Well, perhaps we can have some fun with that."

Savannah was always down for some fun, especially considering how not fun her last few days had been. "What are you thinking?"

"Well, I assume you've noticed the way she keeps looking at you."

"Of course. I've been prancing around the house in my underwear. You should see her when she's trying her best not to look and failing miserably. But it hasn't put her off."

"Then how about you have a wardrobe malfunction today? It wouldn't be the first time someone's breasts have fallen out of those tight corsets they make us wear."

Now that was a good idea. Savannah knew there was a reason she liked working with Amelia. "That's perfect. I'll go to Gray to get her help tucking myself back into the corset."

Amelia chuckled. "That'll be quite something to see."

Engineering an incident wasn't difficult. As Amelia said, the corsets were very tight, and her boobs were practically spilling out of the thing anyway. All it took was Savannah leaning over just a bit too far, and her breasts were free.

"Whoops!" She straightened up and undid the corset, which fastened at the front. "Help me with this, would you, Gray?" She stood boldly in front of

Gray, merely inches away from her with her breasts fully exposed.

Gray took a graceful step back. Her eyes widened and went straight to Savannah's nipples. They were definitely a grey color Savannah noticed. They seemed a pale grey in the artificial lights of the studio.

"I'll leave that to the professionals." Gray looked panicked, but only for a second before she regained composure. One of the costuming ladies was already hurrying over, her quick hands working to refasten the corset, but Savannah wasn't paying attention to her. She was relishing the look of discomfort on Gray's face.

She wasn't usually a vindictive person, but she had no sympathy for someone who had agreed to spy on her for money. And, well, part of her got off on it. Gray was wearing a white T shirt today, it was tight around her arms and Savannah could see her nipples erect though her sports bra and shirt.

Mmmmm. Why is this woman so goddamn sexy.

Savannah had definitely imagined Gray taking hold of her with those strong arms, pinning her down and fucking her hard. The thought crossed her mind pretty often.

The rest of the shoot went without a hitch,

leaving Savannah frustrated. Sexually and otherwise. Gray was still here, showing no signs of leaving. What did Savannah have to do to chase her
off? Maybe if she forced Gray to witness her having
sex, that would be too much and Gray would
finally leave.

"I'm going clubbing," she told Gray cheerfully
after the shoot. "I'll probably be out late, maybe
until two."

"I don't think that's a good idea, Savannah.
Clubs are very public places. It could be dangerous. I think you should keep a low profile until I
manage to find whoever is trying to hurt you."

Savannah didn't waste her breath by
reminding Gray that she wasn't actually in any real
danger. "You don't have to come, if you don't want
to, but I'm going."

Gray sighed. "No, if you're going, then I'm
going."

Savannah wondered what time Gray usually
went to bed. Maybe if she could keep Gray up late
enough, that would help make her more irritable
and thus more susceptible to reaching her
breaking point later when Savannah put her plan
into action.

When Savannah got to the club, she immediately hailed a few friends at the bar. She got a drink for herself—Gray refused to drink anything other than water—and downed it before going onto the dance floor.

Unsurprisingly, Gray followed.

Savannah grinned as she pulled Gray up close, dancing with her so that their bodies moved together as one. Gray's hard muscular body was tight against her own.

She was surprised by her own reaction to Gray's closeness. She felt her heartrate speeding up and was taken by the sudden desire to kiss Gray. She wondered what it would be like to feel Gray's hand between her legs and almost moaned at the thought.

Savannah shut down that line of thought as quickly as she was able to. She was supposed to be chasing Gray off, not giving her reasons to stay. She moved away from Gray, but Gray followed, never letting Savannah out of her sight.

Savannah did her best to forget about Gray, but it was difficult with the way Gray's body moved easily and elegantly to the music. She found herself forgetting all about her plan and making excuses for why it would be okay to get Gray into bed.

Savannah forced herself to go back to the bar and get another drink. Off the dance floor, and away from Gray's seductive movements, her head cleared somewhat and she remembered why she was here. Right. Get rid of Gray.

Savannah surveyed the dance floor and picked out the woman who looked least like Gray she could find. She approached her and started dancing with her. The woman easily took to the movement.

"I'm Savannah."

"Natalie. It's nice to meet you, Savannah."

They danced for a while before Savannah took Natalie by the hand and led her to the bar. "Can I get you a drink?"

"I'd love that."

"You know, it's rather noisy in here. what would you say to a drink at my place?"

Natalie nodded eagerly. "You're right, it is noisy. Let's get out of here."

Savannah didn't signal to Gray that she was leaving, but Gray was keeping an annoyingly close watch on her and wasn't more than a few steps behind her.

As soon as they were all settled in the back of the car, Savannah started kissing Natalie. Natalie returned the kiss enthusiastically for several minutes before breaking away and reaching to the front seat for Gray.

"We're not ignoring you, my dear. Come here."

She made to hold Gray's arm, but Gray caught her wrist and stopped her. "I'm not here for that. I'm Savannah's bodyguard, nothing more."

"Oh," Natalie pouted. "Too bad—we could have had fun."

Savannah was doing her best not to laugh, but it was difficult. This whole thing couldn't have gone better if she'd hired Natalie to act the role. Gray was looking super uncomfortable as she stared pointedly out of the window, and Savannah was already fantasizing about Gray sending Simon her letter of resignation when they got home.

Natalie shrugged and went back to kissing Savannah. Savannah quickly lost herself in the kiss and started groping Natalie.

By the time they got home, both she and Natalie were shirtless and grinding against each other. Gray got out of the car the moment it stopped and held the door open for them. Savannah left her shirt in the car, rubbing Natalie's nipple as they got out.

Natalie moaned and ducked her head into Savannah's neck, sucking a wet kiss to her skin.

Gray followed their excruciatingly slow progress to the bedroom. They undressed along the way, leaving a trail of clothes behind them. By the time Savannah was shutting the door in Gray's face, she and Natalie were both fully naked. The last thing Gray would have seen was Savannah pushing two fingers into Natalie's pussy.

Savannah proceeded to have loud, vigorous sex with Natalie. Knowing that Gray was standing just outside the door, listening to everything, turned her on more than she would have believed possible. She found herself wishing that Gray had taken Natalie up on her offer for a threesome. She would much rather be making Gray cry out in pleasure than making Gray listen to her cries of pleasure.

Of course, that would run completely counter to her plan. Not that Gray would agree even if Savannah did invite her in. She'd made it clear that while she was interested in Savannah, she wasn't going to act on that interest.

Savannah did her best not to think about Gray for now. It wasn't difficult when Natalie was right here in front of her, deliciously wet and tantalizingly beautiful.

After their loud climaxes, they cuddled for a while before Natalie got up, saying she should get going. Savannah made a point of walking through the house naked to collect Natalie's clothes and hand them to her.

To her indignation, Gray was nowhere to be found. She had probably gone to bed. It was late, after all. Savannah was sure that Gray had done her usual nightly check of all the security cameras before lying down and rolled her eyes at the thought.

As much as she wanted to sleep in the next day, she set her alarm early, determined to drag Gray out on another long shopping trip. Perhaps if she could wake Gray early enough, she'd be tired and cranky enough to finally give up and leave.

Unfortunately, that part of the plan backfired.

It seemed that Gray could function perfectly well on less sleep. Maybe it was an army thing?

Savannah, however, was tired and cranky, and didn't enjoy the shopping nearly as much as she usually would have. Still, she persevered, just to see if she could get Gray to crack.

She gave up after several hours and steered them toward the fanciest restaurant she could find. She knew she would fit in with her designer clothes, but Gray was hopelessly underdressed. Savannah hoped to make her uncomfortable somewhere where she clearly didn't fit in.

"Savannah, going to this restaurant is a bad idea. It's too public. You'll be exposed."

"Don't be such a worrywart. The club last night was fine, wasn't it?"

"Just because the club was fine doesn't mean that the restaurant will be. It's not worth the risk."

"That's for me to decide, isn't it? Come along now," Savannah said airily.

Gray was practically gnashing her teeth in frustration, but she followed Savannah without any further comment. Savannah sat down and ordered for both of them without asking Gray what she wanted.

Gray caught the waiter's arm as he passed. "Actually, I'd like the tomato soup, not the salmon."

Savannah scowled, but she didn't press the point. The food came and Savannah dug in.

Gray's eyes were constantly moving as she scanned the guests at the restaurant. She didn't seem to care that she was underdressed. Nobody else seemed to care either.

Savannah ate her food sulkily, thinking longingly of her bed. She was definitely taking a nap when she got home.

She paid as soon as she and Gray were done and walked back to the car without really paying attention to her surroundings.

Gray was paying attention to her surroundings, and that's what saved her.

"Savannah!" Gray grabbed Savannah's arm and yanked hard as a gunshot rang out in the still air. Savannah spun around, staring in shock as a black, windowless van pulled up. Four men with guns advanced on her and Gray.

Savannah froze, terror pounding through her veins. Was this going to be how she died?

Gray didn't freeze. She kept a tight grip on Savannah's hand and pulled back into the restaurant. Savannah could do nothing but try to keep up as Gray practically flew through the kitchen and out of the back door.

She was already on her phone with her free hand. "Tony, we're out back. Come around and pick us up, now!"

Moments later, Tony brought their car around and Gray shoved Savannah into the back seat, diving in after her. Gray's hard body was on top of her momentarily, pressed into her, her weight a reassuring presence on top of Savannah before Gray extracted herself and sat up. Savannah felt scared. She wanted to pull Gray back on top of her.

"Drive, drive! Head south, as fast as you can."

The car screeched away. Gray turned around to look through the back window. "I think we've lost them," she murmured after a few moments. "They didn't realize that there was a back entrance and were expecting us to have to come out from the front. By the time they figured out that we'd found another way out, we were already gone. Good thing I researched the layouts of all the restaurants in the area, just in case."

Savannah could only admire Gray's dedication in silence, because she was still too shocked to speak. Gray finally turned away from the back window, her face settling into an expression of concern as she took in Savannah's pale face and shaking hands.

"Savannah, are you alright?"

"Th-they tried to kill me."

"They weren't trying to kill you. That shot was aimed at your leg. They wanted to disable you or scare you before they kidnapped you."

"Oh, like that's so much better! I've got people

who want to fucking kidnap me running around with guns!"

"That's what I'm here for," Gray said patiently and she looked at her with those intense grey eyes. "I'll protect you, I promise."

Savannah stared at Gray. She felt tears forming in the corners of her eyes. She had been wrong. This wasn't a power play by her father after all. She truly was in danger.

Gray had just saved her life, even after all the crap Savannah had put her through. Savannah felt terrible. If she'd been in Gray's position, she'd have been tempted to let the kidnappers have their way out of sheer frustration.

"Just try to breathe. You're safe now. We're nearly home. No one is going to get to you there."

Savannah nodded, grateful for the first time for all the security measures Gray had put in. Savannah had thought they were unnecessary, but now she was glad that Gray had insisted on going ahead, even without her approval.

Savannah didn't move at first when the car stopped. Gray came around to her side and opened the door for her.

"Come on, Savannah," she said quietly. "Let's get you inside."

She drew Savannah out of the car and put an arm around her. Savannah shrank into Gray's embrace, letting Gray lead her quickly across the lawn and inside.

"How do I know I'm safe here?" Savannah had thought that she would feel safe once she was inside, but she was still jittery and anxious. "What if they know where I live?"

"Come with me."

Savannah followed Gray through one of the seldom-used guest rooms. It had been completely converted into a surveillance room.

"Look here. There are cameras on every corner of the grounds. After the incident just now, I'm going to search the house, and then I'm going to spend the next couple of hours in here, watching the cameras, just in case. There are also alarms, which I'm going to set now, so that even if I miss something on camera, those will go off. If a cat so much as jumps onto the wall, we'll know about it."

Savannah took a shaky breath and nodded. Gray really did know what she was doing. "I think I need to lie down."

"You do that. I'll just search your room first."

For once, Savannah didn't protest. She waited for Gray to finish her search before crawling into bed and pulling the covers over her head. She closed her eyes and tried not to see the men with guns.

Savannah couldn't believe Gray was being so kind after Savannah had been so awful to her. She wanted to thank Gray somehow, but words just didn't seem like enough.

She wanted to do something to show Gray that she was sincere, when everything she had done so far had led Gray to believe that she was incapable of sincerity.

An idea struck her. Savannah got out of bed and walked quickly to her studio. She always kept that door locked, not wanting anyone to judge her for her true passion. Gray wouldn't judge her, though. Maybe Gray would even appreciate having a small painting as a gesture of Savannah's gratitude. It was the best idea Savannah could come up with.

She got out a little canvas and started mixing paints.

6
GRAY

Gray was fuming. She had learned during her time in the army how to keep her emotions under control, even when she was furious. She had comforted and reassured Savannah, as was her duty to her client, even though all she felt like doing was shouting in Savannah's stupid, stubborn face.

Savannah had done nothing but fight her tooth and nail from the start. Gray had *told* her not to go to the restaurant, and now Savannah was all shocked that something had happened? Well, Gray hoped that she had learned her lesson. Maybe Savannah would actually listen to her in future.

The worst of it was that she knew her current frustration wasn't entirely directed toward Savannah. Gray was almost just as frustrated with herself. She hated how she was constantly drawn to Savannah. Savannah was stupidly tempting, always in a bikini or underwear when at home. And now she had seen her naked, images of her nipples, her lovely brown big nipples, were constantly flashing through Gray's mind too. She only briefly caught a glance of Savannah fully nude, but she wouldn't ever forget that triangle of golden blonde pubic hair between her legs.

Gray had managed to avoid masturbating to the thought of her again, but that had just left her frustrated and resentful of the effect Savannah had on her.

She paced up and down in the surveillance room, keeping a careful eye on the cameras. She doubted the kidnappers would try to take Savannah here, it would be much easier for them in a public place, but she still had to be vigilant, just in case.

At least they did seem to be trying to kidnap her rather than kill her. That shot was at the ground, meant to shock and paralyse them so that they could get Savannah into the van. That would make Gray's job a little easier, if she didn't have to defend against lethal force. Savannah certainly wasn't making it easy for her; it was about time the universe cut her a break.

There was a flicker of movement on the cameras, but it was just a bird. Gray took her hand off her gun, forcing herself to take a settling breath. It surprised her to realize how upsetting she found the idea of anything happening to Savannah.

Of course, she cared about all of her clients' safety and didn't want any of them to get hurt, but the idea of someone taking Savannah against her will felt like Gray had been hit in the stomach with a block of ice.

She had seen Savannah's vulnerable side today, her mask had slipped and underneath she was a sweet and scared girl that Gray felt driven to protect.

She quickly dismissed the thought of anyone taking Savannah. She wasn't going to let anyone take Savannah, so it wasn't going to be an issue.

Gray kept an eye on the cameras for several hours before venturing out for dinner. Surprisingly, Savannah wasn't in the dining room. She had never missed dinner before and Gray was instantly worried. Was Savannah more upset than Gray had realized? Gray didn't like to think of her hiding in her room, too scared to come out.

Her appetite suddenly gone, Gray pushed her food away and stood up. She went to Savannah's room. The door was open, but Savannah wasn't there. Gray forced down an irrational spike of panic. No alarms had been triggered. There wasn't any way anyone could have taken Savannah. She had simply moved to a different part of the house. That had to be it.

Gray checked in the bathroom before starting a methodical search of the house. Unfortunately, Savannah's house was huge, and by the time Gray was approaching the last few rooms she hadn't looked in yet, she was becoming seriously concerned.

She was just considering trying to call Savannah to see if she had her cell phone on her when Savannah stepped out of a room that had always been locked before. Gray hadn't been able to gain access, even when citing security reasons.

Savannah was holding something small and square close to her chest. She turned and locked the door to the room and turned back to the corridor, squeaking in surprise when she saw Gray.

"Sorry, I didn't mean to startle you. You had me worried; I didn't know where you had gone."

Gray expected Savannah to roll her eyes and make some comment about her presence being unnecessary, but instead, Savannah dipped her head slightly and spoke in an apologetic tone.

"I guess I should have told you that I was leaving my room. I didn't mean to alarm you."

Gray was so taken aback by the almost-apology that she was left staring dumbly at Savannah. Where had this sweet, humble Savannah come from? She had no idea, but she certainly wasn't complaining about the temporary absence of the spoiled brat who did everything she could to get under Gray's skin.

"Do—do you want to have a drink with me?"

Well, things just got stranger and stranger.

"Sure," Gray said in a strangled voice.

She followed Savannah to her room, well aware of how many people Savannah must have had sex within this room. It didn't help when Savannah perched on the edge of the bed, the picture of beauty and elegance. Her long blonde hair spilled down over her shoulders and onto her breasts.

Fuck, Gray had it bad.

"I made you something."

Savannah held out the square thing, which turned out to be a small canvas. On it was painted the most beautiful rose that Gray had ever seen. It took her breath away with its bright colors and elegant sweeps of petals enfolding themselves into one cohesive flower. Each of the petals was a different color, but instead of clashing, it simply made the rose look like someone had picked a piece of the rainbow.

"It's beautiful," she breathed. "You painted this?"

Savannah's eyes dropped to the ground. "I know it's not exactly an appropriate hobby for someone of my station." Her cheeks went red, and she wouldn't meet Gray's gaze.

"Hey." Gray gently titled Savannah's chin up until Savannah was looking at her. "You should be able to do whatever you want to do, station be damned. You're so talented—you don't want to waste a gift like this."

"You think so?"

"Absolutely."

By the sparkling, grateful smile Savannah gave her, Gray suspected that these were the first words of encouragement Savannah had ever heard for her painting. Gray wanted to get hold of whoever had discouraged Savannah from following her passion and slam them into a wall.

Savannah poured two glasses of champagne and handed one to Gray.

"Champagne, huh? What are we celebrating?"

"My not being kidnapped today."

Gray chuckled. "That's certainly something to celebrate."

They toasted and drank. Savannah pulled on a seductive smile, one Gray had seen many times, though it had never been directed at her.

"You were so sexy today," Savannah purred, leaning close to her. "There's nothing so hot as a woman who takes control of a situation."

Gray wanted to take control of the situation now. She wanted to grab Savannah and kiss her senseless. She wanted to thoroughly ravage her and make her scream louder than any of those other women Savannah had slept with ever had.

She couldn't, though. Savannah was a client, she reminded herself. She was not going to sleep with a client. She decided it was best to change the subject.

"How long have you been painting?"

"Ever since school. I took art classes, but never pursued them after school. I wanted to, but my father disapproved."

"You care for his approval."

Savannah shrugged. "Not really, but I need to be careful. He has control of my trust fund. If I piss him off too much, he can pull funding at any time. The thing with the art classes came at a time when I was going out and getting drunk a lot. He had to pull quite a few strings to get me out of a number of sticky situations and was not in a tolerant mood. I thought it best not to push for the classes, so I continued on my own."

"You must have a lot of natural talent, then, to have achieved what you have without further teaching." Gray looked again at the rose. "This truly is beautiful. How in the world did you get it to dry so fast?"

Savannah grinned. "I used a hair dryer. There are a lot of tips and tricks online if you look for them."

"Have you ever considered selling your art?

That could be a way to earn an income independent of your father."

Savannah looked honestly surprised by the idea. "I—no, I hadn't considered it. There are so many good artists out there; I don't see how my work would really stand out."

"Trust me, it would stand out. I'm not an art connoisseur, but one of my previous clients owns an art gallery. If you'd like, I can get him to look at some of your pieces and give you a professional opinion on whether it's something you might be able to pursue as a career."

Savannah nodded eagerly, her eyes shining in a way Gray hadn't ever seen them shine before. "That would be amazing! This house is in my name, so all I'd really need to be free of my father is a regular income. If my painting could provide that..."

Gray couldn't imagine what it must be like to live under someone else's control. "I'll talk to my contact," she promised.

"Thanks, Gray. You do such a good job of taking care of me." Her big blue eyes looked up at Gray, all innocence and loveliness.

Gray shrugged, well aware of the way

Savannah was batting her eyelashes at her. "It's my job."

"Do you always go above and beyond for your clients?"

"I always do my very best. That's why I got into this industry."

"So noble. What about before? You were in the army, right?"

"That's right. Some of my old army buddies think I'm crazy to be in private security, what with the stories I've told them, but it's a hell of a lot less stressful than active duty."

"I bet all the crap I've put you through is going to make a good story, huh?"

Gray had to chuckle at that. "Yeah, you'll definitely be a story all on your own."

"I'm sorry, Gray. I thought my father sent you to spy on me."

"I wouldn't do that. Your father might be paying me, but I'm not reporting back to him on anything."

"Anything? You haven't told him about the attack today?"

Gray shook her head. "You're my client. That's up to you."

She knew it was a dangerous line she was walking. If she pissed Simon off, he could pull funding for the job, but she would rather lose the job than betray Savannah's confidence. At this point, Gray thought she might even continue to guard Savannah for free if necessary. She needed Savannah to be alright, though she still didn't understand what it was about Savannah that was so compelling.

Seeing this other side to her and sharing the first pleasant conversation they'd had since Gray had arrived only served to deepen both her attraction and the draw Savannah had on her.

Savannah leaned in close. She must be wearing some kind of perfume, because she smelled unfairly good, like roses and lavender and something else Gray couldn't quite place. "I don't know what I would have done without you today, Gray," she murmured.

Gray wanted to kiss her. She wanted it so badly it hurt, and her reasons for not doing it were swiftly vanishing from her mind.

Savannah's gaze flicked down to Gray's lips.

Gray broke. She leaned in, capturing Savannah's lips in a kiss. Savannah moaned and returned the kiss passionately, thrusting her tongue into Gray's mouth, licking into her in a way that sent shivers down Gray's spine.

Gray kissed Savannah back like she was suffocating and Savannah was oxygen. Her hands were tangled in Savannah's hair and Savannah's hands were resting on Gray's hips, pulling her in closer.

The kiss was so heated that Gray vaguely wondered why the furniture around them wasn't smoking, why she and Savannah weren't combusting through the passion of their connection. Savannah was everything and Gray couldn't get enough of her.

Gray was seconds way from ripping Savannah's clothes off when reality came crashing back in.

What the fuck was she doing? Savannah was a client. She couldn't do this.

It was almost physically painful to wrench herself away from Savannah, but Gray did it.

She gasped for breath, her body still tingling from the aftereffects of the kiss. "We—it's late. We should get to bed," Gray gasped.

It wasn't late. It was barely even dinner time yet, but Gray needed to remove herself from the situation before she did something irreversible.

"Gray, wait –"

Gray couldn't afford to wait to hear what

Savannah had to say. She had to get out of here *now*.

She practically fled the scene and locked herself in her room, thanking whatever higher powers were listening that Savannah didn't follow her. Gray didn't think she'd have been able to resist her if she had.

Gray sank to the floor in her room with her back against the door. What had she done? She'd gone and kissed her client, that's what she'd done, and there was no taking that back. Would Savannah be furious? She had every right to be. She was scared and vulnerable right now, and Gray had taken advantage of that.

Gray felt sickened with herself. There were so many things wrong with this situation. Would Savannah have kissed her back if she hadn't still been feeling grateful to Gray for saving her life? Gray couldn't say for sure that she would have, and she hated herself for putting Savannah in that position.

What would this mean for her business, if word got out? She had always prided herself on being professional, but this was the very height of unprofessional behavior.

And of course, there was Amelia...

Gray knew that Amelia would want her to be happy, but she still felt like kissing Savannah was a betrayal of her past love. She hadn't been with anyone else for so long, and Savannah was so different from Amelia. It felt like Gray was spitting in Amelia's face by even contemplating being with Savannah.

Gray seldom cried, but now, she felt tears streaking down her face. She'd messed everything up so badly. Would Savannah even want Gray to guard her anymore? She could continue guarding Savannah even if Simon pulled funding, but not if Savannah withdrew consent. Without Savannah's consent, she would be nothing more than an intruder for the police to remove.

Gray would have to convince Savannah to allow someone else from her company to take over Gray's guarding duties, even if she didn't want Gray herself. The alternative was unthinkable. Though if there was any way she could stay on herself, she wanted to be the one to ensure Savannah's safety for reasons she couldn't quite put into words.

She'd wait until tomorrow before approaching Savannah to apologize, once her head was clearer.

Hopefully, they could move past her blunder and she would be able to stay on.

Of course, that would do little to erase the bubbling guilt in Gray's chest.

She tossed and turned that night, only falling asleep sometime near dawn, and when she did, she had troubled dreams of Savannah.

7

SAVANNAH

Savannah stared after Gray. For the second time today, she was too shocked to move. She had never been rejected by a woman. Never and *Gray* had the nerve to turn her down? Shock was quickly turning to outrage.

How dare Gray reject her like that? Did she not realize how many people were vying to be with Savannah? When would she ever get a chance to be with someone as beautiful and seductive as Savannah? Few people ever got that chance. Savannah knew that she was talented in bed— she'd had plenty of practice at it. She could please Gray like no other woman could, and Gray had just... turned her down? It didn't make any sense.

Savannah considered running after Gray but decided that she had more dignity than that. She wouldn't beg for anyone's attention, not even Gray's. Gray would have to come to her sooner or later—she was Savannah's bodyguard, after all.

Gray didn't emerge from her room for dinner, so Savannah ate alone. It felt strange to be without Gray's constant presence, and she hated herself slightly for missing it.

Well, she was just going to show Gray exactly what she was missing. Had Gray thought Savannah was flaunting herself before? Well now, Savannah was going to pull out all the stops.

She went to bed late, staying up to message people to arrange her plans for tomorrow. She needed to message the right people—people who didn't mind having sex in front of a bodyguard. Gray didn't want her? Fine. Let her see exactly what she was missing and still claim she didn't want Savannah.

Savannah went to bed with her head buzzing with plans and woke up the next day feeling antsy and unrested.

Breakfast was eaten in uncomfortable silence. Savannah wondered if Gray was going to ignore the whole incident entirely. That seemed unlike her. Gray was the sort of person to tackle things head on.

Sure enough, as soon as their plates were cleared, Gray fixed Savannah with a steely gaze. "Savannah, we need to talk. I'm—"

Just then, the doorbell rang. "I'll get it." Savannah didn't particularly care for whatever Gray had to say, and she was eager to get her plan moving. She couldn't wait to see Gray go green with jealousy, or red with embarrassment, or some shade of purple as she fought to stop herself from joining in.

Lily, Cara and Kimberly were all dressed in bathing suits with transparent cover ups, giggling slightly.

"Welcome, ladies. The pool is this way. I'll be with your shortly."

Gray followed Savannah to her room, though turned pointedly away when Savannah started stripping, quickly changing into her sexiest bikini —not that she intended to keep it on for long. She grabbed her box of toys and took it with her, dropping it on the deck in plain sight. Gray glanced at it once before gazing deliberately in another direction.

Savannah paid no attention to Gray as she

sauntered over to the pool and slipped into the water, coming up behind Kimberly, wrapping her arms around Kimberly's slim waist.

Kimberly smiled and tilted her head back, allowing Savannah to start pressing kisses to her neck. Savannah performed a loud moan as Lily came up behind her and wrapped her arms around Savannah, her fingers going to Savannah's nipples. Kimberly was reaching for Cara's clit under the water, and Cara's cries were music to Savannah's ears.

They moved from the pool to the deck, lying down on spread out towels, hands and tongues everywhere. Savannah glanced up to see Gray's eyes on her. Gray's face was flushed and she didn't break Savannah's gaze.

Fuck, that was so hot. Savannah looked right at Gray as Kimberly used a strap on to push a dildo into her pussy.

Gray finally broke, looking away. Savannah grinned in satisfaction as she cried out on the dildo, thrusting back into it. Cara started kissing her, and Savannah reached down for Cara's breasts with her free hand. Lily was fucking Kimberly from behind with a second strap on.

It was the perfect orgy, and the perfect torture for Gray. She was indeed a strange mixture of red and purple and Savannah loved it.

She spent the rest of the day with Kimberly, Lily and Cara. They were in and out of the pool, and in and out of each other. Savannah lost track of how many times she came or had another woman come on her tongue or fingers. It was a thoroughly good day, just what she needed to cleanse herself of last night. And if it taught Gray a lesson in what she had missed out on, so much the better.

Dinner was even more awkward than breakfast had been. Savannah had taken lunch by the pool and Gray had had a tray brought out for herself. Lily, Cara and Kimberly elected not to stay the night. All four of them were so thoroughly fucked that Savannah thought another round might just kill them.

So, she and Gray ate alone. She wondered if Gray would try to reprimand her for her scandalous behavior. Just let her try...

"Savannah, I need to apologize."

"What?" That certainly wasn't what she had been expecting.

"I was wrong to kiss you. You're a client and it's unprofessional. Not only that but you were still scared and vulnerable after the attack, and I never should have taken advantage of you in the way I did. I hope that we can move on from this and continue to work together."

Savannah softened, suddenly regretting what she had put Gray through today, remembering how Gray had saved her life only the day before. "You don't need to apologize, Gray. You weren't taking advantage of me. I wanted it just as much as you did."

She just wished Gray hadn't pulled away, but she wasn't going to admit that.

Gray sighed softly. "Thank you for saying that. I promise, it won't happen again."

Savannah couldn't help pouting. "What if I want it to happen again?"

"It can't, Savannah. You're my client. It's not right."

"It certainly felt right last night."

Gray closed her eyes for a moment. "You're going to be the death of me," she murmured. "You sweet, seductive creature."

Savannah preened under the praise. She decided that she wanted to be exactly that—seductive. She was going to seduce Gray, no matter what it took.

Of course, she'd need to be careful. She didn't want to ruin her public image. She'd spent years cultivating that image and didn't want to let it go just yet. People saw her as just another brainless rich model with nothing between her ears.

Savannah wanted people to think that. It was easy to be dismissed that way, and if people weren't paying attention to her, she could spend more time painting and less time doing the things that were expected of someone of her station.

Savannah liked the perks of being rich, to be sure, but she craved a life of more substance. Of course, her father wouldn't take well to hearing that. He wanted her to be a pretty little thing that he could show off at work functions and nothing more.

No one really understood what it was like to live a life you were only half-invested in. Savannah didn't dare chase her dreams, not when the whole world seemed set on seeing her behave a certain way.

Gray seemed to understand, though. Gray had even offered to help her, which was more than anyone else ever had.

This just made Savannah even more determined to have her. Gray was good at what she did.
Sooner or later, Gray would find and end the
threat to Savannah's life, and then she would have
no reason to stay... unless Savannah gave her one.

It was strange, but even though she was still
indignant about yesterday's rejection, the thought
of not having Gray in her life filled Savannah with
panic, and not panic related to her safety. She
couldn't imagine going about her day without
Gray's soothing presence, as much as she hated to
admit that to herself.

"I want to go out tomorrow. I hate being cooped
up in the house. Is there somewhere that you think
might be safer for me to go?" The last thing Savannah
wanted was a repeat of yesterday's near-kidnapping.

"Thank you for asking. There's a small
boutique nail bar not far from here. It's isolated
and takes clients by appointments only. You could
go for a manicure, if you'd like."

"That's... actually a really good idea. How did
you even find out about that place? You don't seem
like the type to get your nails done."

"I'm not, but I've been looking into safer
options for public activities. I was hoping to tempt

you with one next time you wanted to go clubbing, or shopping, or out for a meal."

Not for the first time, Savannah admired the dedication Gray put into her work. "Well, a manicure sounds perfect. We can both have one."

"That's not necess—"

"I insist. My treat."

Gray sighed. "If it'll save me from another shopping trip, then I guess it's a small price to pay."

Savannah chuckled. "I've done quite a lot of shopping recently, even for me. I think I'm good to go for a while."

"That's a relief to hear. Are you ready for bed? I'd like to check the house on more time before we retire."

"So ready to take me to bed, Gray? At least offer me a drink, first." Savannah gave Gray her flirtiest wink. Gray blushed slightly but didn't otherwise react.

"Let me check your room before you go in."

Savannah started undressing while Gray was checking her room, but Gray remained infuriatingly professional, her eyes barely skating over Savannah as she checked inside the closet, under the bed, and in every other conceivable location where an intruder could be hiding.

A few days ago, Savannah would have rolled her eyes and grouched about how all this was unnecessary. Now, it made her feel safe and she was glad for Gray's thoroughness.

When Gray was finished checking the room, Savannah lay down facing her. "I'm cold, Gray. Hand me another blanket."

Gray huffed but handed Savannah the blanket regardless. Savannah caught Gray's hand in hers, rubbing her thumbs across Gray's knuckles. "You know, I can think of a better way to get warm," she purred, pressing a wet kiss to the back of Gray's hand.

She was sure she wasn't imagining the hitch in Gray's breath, but Gray carefully removed her hand and stepped back. "I'll turn up the heat on my way past when I'm checking the rest of the house."

So, she was going to be stubborn about this. Well, Savannah could be stubborn, too. She had never yet met a woman able to resist her. She would seduce Gray eventually, one way or another.

The next day, they went to the nail bar. Savannah got hers done in a sparkling, glittery pink. She managed to persuade Gray to get a black polish on her neat short nails. Gray had laughed and given into her desires.

They didn't talk much during the manicure. Gray tried to start conversation several times, but Savannah was all too aware that there were people watching them. It was easy to slip into her previous bratty behavior with Gray. Savannah complained loudly about how boring it was to have a body-guard follow her everywhere and whined about when she would be free to go to clubs and restaurants again.

Gray didn't call her out on her sudden change of attitude. She answered Savannah's questions patiently, explaining that Savannah could go out again as soon as the threat against her was resolved. In all honesty, Savannah wasn't keen on doing anything Gray considered risky until Gray said it was safe, but she had an image to keep up, after all.

She knew Gray well enough to tell that Gray was annoyed, but Gray hid it well, her only tell being a slight twitch in her left eyebrow every time Savannah started moaning about something new.

They spent several hours at the nail bar before going home. It had a lounge area where they could get a drink and snack. Savannah was planning to spend the afternoon on the deck sunbathing, but Gray had other plans.

"Why don't you paint for the afternoon? I'll stand guard outside the door and tell anyone who comes by that you're taking a private call. That way, no one will know what you're up to."

Savannah looked at Gray in surprise. The idea certainly was appealing. It wasn't a secret that she painted, but she was self-conscious about it and didn't like to draw too much attention to it.

"That... That would be great. Thank you, Gray." Savannah pushed down a wave of guilt for how frostily she had behaved with Gray earlier today. She would make it up to Gray later.

She quickly lost herself in the act of painting, emerging only when Gray knocked on the door to remind her that it was dinner time.

"You may want to take a shower before dinner." Gray gestured at Savannah's front, and on glancing down she realized that she had spots of paint all over her and her clothes.

"Thanks. I suppose our whole ruse would have been for nothing if I'd gone to dinner like this. Did anyone come by?"

"Hannah passed and asked where you were. I gave her the story about the private call."

Savannah nodded. "I'll just take a shower, then. Hold these, would you?"

She started stripping off where she was, handing her clothes to Gray.

Gray grumbled under her breath about Savannah not being able to keep her clothes on if her life depended on it, which made Savannah giggle. She wiggled her ass as she walked to the bathroom, sure that Gray must be watching.

Sure enough, a glance back showed Gray quickly looking away, not quite fast enough to hide where her eyes had been a moment before.

"You sure you don't want to join me?" Savannah asked innocently. "You must be tired from standing all day. I could give you a back rub."

"Tempting, but no." Gray smiled at her. "You're still my client, Savannah."

"You and your rules. You're not fun, Gray."

"Tell me that again when I next save your life."

"Touché."

Savannah went to bed plotting her next move.

Over the next few weeks, they settled into a pattern. Savannah did her best to live her typical rich girl lifestyle, in the limits of what Gray determined was safe. She still went to modeling shoots, but only after Gray had thoroughly scouted the location. They avoided restaurants and malls. Savannah got into online shopping and had her driver go to various restaurants to pick up takeout when she had a craving for something that only a specific restaurant provided.

She was bratty with Gray in public, but in private, she found herself softening and opening up. She even let Gray into her studio. Gray was amazed by the paintings and generous with her praise. Savannah shrugged and brushed it off, but inside she glowed with pride. It felt good to be appreciated for doing something she loved rather than something that was simply expected of her.

They would typically spend the morning out and about, and the afternoons at home painting or simply hanging out. Savannah found that she genuinely liked Gray's company and conversation. Gray had some great stories about her time in the army, and Savannah shared her own recollections of what it was like to grow up as the daughter of a billionaire.

Through it all, Savannah continued in her relentless attempts to seduce Gray. She could tell that Gray was close to cracking. They had been seconds away from kissing several times, but Gray had always pulled back just before their lips met.

Savannah was determined to wear her down. Sooner or later, she would have Gray in her bed. It was only a matter of time.

8

GRAY

Savannah was driving Gray mad. Every day, she got closer and closer to snapping—to pinning Savannah to a wall and kissing her senseless, to tearing her clothes off and fucking her hard. The worst of it was that she knew Savannah wouldn't object. She had made it very clear that she would be an eager participant in such activities, which made it even harder to resist.

To make matters even more difficult, Gray knew by now that this wasn't a reaction to nearly being kidnapped. Savannah was still wary, but she was no longer severely shaken like she had been that first night. Gray was confident that she wasn't simply seeking comfort in Gray's embrace.

However, what she was seeking remained in question. Gray knew that Savannah was stubborn. At first, getting rid of her had been a game to Savannah. Now that Savannah knew she needed Gray, seducing her had become the new game. Savannah wanted to win Gray to her bed as a matter of pride.

Gray didn't want to be some conquest in a long line of conquests. She needed to guard her heart, which meant keeping Savannah out of it. If she gave in, Savannah would surely get bored of her soon—she seldom stayed with one woman for long—and then Gray would be left hurt and abandoned.

It wouldn't matter if it was just casual sex, but she was starting to genuinely care for Savannah. She didn't want to be discarded by her like just another meaningless fling.

It gave her whiplash how Savannah could change from brat one moment to seductress the next. It also hadn't escaped her when the change happened. Savannah clearly wanted to keep up a public image. It was when she and Gray were alone that she became someone different, someone Gray suspected was closer to the true

Savannah, rather than what she was increasingly realizing was a mask.

It was sad that Savannah felt she needed to act the way other people expected of her, but Gray couldn't really blame her. Savannah had grown up with nothing but expectations all around her. Gray had been born into an unremarkable family and had been left to make of her own life what she would. Savannah didn't have that luxury.

Gray hoped that, someday, Savannah would feel comfortable enough to show her true self to the world and not just to Gray, but she was grateful that Savannah felt safe enough with her to be herself, at least.

She loved watching Savannah paint. Gray had contacted Oliver and he was eager to look at Savannah's work after seeing the photo Gray had sent him of the rose Savanah had painted, but Savannah balked when it came to setting down a date.

She was nervous about being judged, and it was taking Gray quite some time to reassure her that Oliver wasn't like that. She was sure she would get through to Savannah eventually, and fortunately, Oliver was a patient man.

More and more, Gray was looking forward to

those quiet afternoons and evenings with Savannah, where they talked about everything and nothing, or sometimes just sat in comfortable, companionable silence. Gray even tried her hand at painting, at Savannah's urging.

She was terrible at it, and the two of them had a great time laughing at some of Gray's more disastrous attempts, including a portrait of Savanah that somehow ended up with three arms and a bust bigger than its head. Savannah had insisted on framing it and putting it up in the studio.

"Gray, won't you help me? My bra has come unstrapped."

Gray was one hundred percent sure that Savannah could manage to fasten her own bra strap, and almost as certain that it hadn't come unstrapped by accident, but she went over to help anyway. It seemed that there was little she could deny Savannah.

She reached carefully under Savannah's shirt and fastened the bra, trying to touch as little skin as possible.

It would be so easy to reach around and caress Savannah's breasts. She knew Savannah wouldn't object.

"Mmm, you feel good." Savannah leaned back

into Gray's touch, tilting her neck back so that her head was resting on Gray's shoulder, at the perfect angle for Gray to press a kiss into the side of her neck.

She's my client, she's my client, she's my client, Gray chanted to herself. It was almost painful to step back, but she did it with willpower she didn't even realize she had. "There you are. Shall we go?"

"Of course," Savannah said brightly, as if nothing out of the ordinary had transpired. For Savannah, Gray supposed that this wasn't really anything out of the ordinary.

This woman was going to be the death of her.

Savannah waited in the car, as usual, while Gray scouted the location for the shoot. It was a bit more open than she would have liked, but as long as she stayed close to Savannah and kept her eyes open, she thought it would be fine. There was a good vantage point just to the right of where the cameras would be. Gray could perch herself there and keep watch.

Thankfully, this wasn't another swimsuit shoot. Gray thought that she might just lose it if she had to watch Savannah rub lotion onto her body around a tiny bikini again. Unfortunately, she still had to watch Savannah strip unashamedly and change into the long, slinky dress that she would be modeling.

Gray did her best to keep her eyes on Savannah's face... and failed miserably. The worst was when Savannah caught her looking, but Savannah never called her out on her unprofessional behavior. She simply smiled knowingly and wiggled her ass or did something else to drive Gray mad.

The shoot was long, as shoots always were. Gray could tell that Savannah was bored, but only because she was coming to know her so well. From the outside, Savannah appeared engaged, laughing and chatting with the other models, ignoring Gray entirely. There was no sparkle in her eyes, though.

Gray knew she was thinking about what she'd do when she got home. Savannah had been talking about doing a series of flower paintings. She and Gray had accordingly spent many hours in flower shops recently. Savannah had hired a professional photographer to take some photos of the flowers— for a fee paid to the shop owners, of course—and had them printed out on canvas as inspiration for the paintings she wanted to do.

Gray loved how Savannah incorporated at least some small rainbow portion into everything she painted. She loved how out and proud Savannah was. During her time in the army, it had been in the midst of Don't Ask. Don't Tell. Gray had been forced to keep her sexuality secret. Only those closest to her and Amelia had known that they were in a relationship.

Savannah was like one of those ancient sex goddesses who practically oozed seduction and the promise of carnal pleasures. Gray knew first-hand from listening in on far too many intimate moments that Savannah always fulfilled those promises.

When the shoot was finished, Savannah was tired and trudged alongside Gray to the car. Gray was tired too, but she didn't let her vigilance wane.

She caught sight of the van as it turned the corner and stiffened. It was black and windowless, just like the one that had come at Savannah a few weeks ago. She grabbed Savannah's hand and made to pull her back into the building where they had done the shoot, but before she could, an unremarkable man who had appeared to be just passing by suddenly pulled out a gun and pointed it at Savannah.

"Don't move," he snarled. "Get in the van."

A quick glance showed that the van was almost

upon them. Gray knew that she had to act now, before backup arrived.

She lunged for the gun, grabbing the man's wrist and twisting it until it made a loud cracking noise. He fell to his knees, screaming, as Gray confiscated his gun. The doors to the van opened and Gray put herself in front of Savannah, shooting at the masked figures, keeping track of the now-unarmed man beside her as he staggered to a standing position and ran away. Despite the chaos surrounding her, Gray fired with expertise and one of the van's occupants cried out and fell forward onto the sidewalk.

The van kept going, clearly judging it too risky to continue with Gray shooting at them, leaving their man bleeding on the sidewalk.

Savannah was screaming hysterically, and Gray turned automatically to comfort her. "Savannah, it's okay." She put her hands on Savannah's shoulders, squeezing gently. "You're alright, sweetheart. Just breathe for me. They're gone." Except for the guy she'd shot, who Gray would be taking to the police for questioning. Once they had him, it wouldn't take them long to link him to Herom, and then the threat to Savannah's safety would be over.

Savannah threw herself into Gray's arms,

sobbing. Gray hugged her tightly, murmuring soothing words in her ear. After a few minutes, Savannah calmed somewhat and Gray gently extracted herself from their embrace. "Go inside, Savannah. I'm going to deal with this."

"I don't want to leave you! It's not safe."

It was safer for Savannah inside, but Gray could well understand her not feeling safe alone.

"Alright but stay back and keep an eye on the street."

"I will."

Gray turned back to the man on the street... to find nothing but a blood stain.

Shit. Gray had thought he was unconscious. Clearly, she had been wrong.

She followed the drops of blood at a jog, quickly spotting the man at the end of the street. He was being helped into the black van by one of his companions. Gray shot at the van again, but it was too late. The door was already closing and it was driving away. Her shots bounced harmlessly off it.

"Fuck. FUCK!" What the hell had she done? She'd let her feelings get in the way of her job, that's what. She'd been more concerned with comforting Savannah than taking the steps needed to ensure her safety in the long term. Savannah had been hysterical, but she'd been in no immediate danger.

If Gray had just ignored her for a few minutes to ensure that the man she had shot was really unconscious—and restrained him when she realized he wasn't—he would be on his way to the police station right now. Savannah would have had to endure a few more minutes of panic, but the threat to her life would be close to being resolved. Now, it was no closer to being resolved, and it was all Gray's fault.

She had always prided herself on doing her job to the best of her abilities. She didn't always succeed at everything she attempted, but she always put her all into it and did everything she could to protect her clients.

Today had not been her best. She had let herself become emotionally compromised, and Savannah was still in danger because of it.

Gray turned to Savannah to apologize, but Savannah threw herself once more into Gray's arms. "Thank you. You saved me—again."

"Don't thank me," Gray muttered. "I let him get away. I was stupid. I should have stopped him."

"You saved me; that's what counts. I don't know what I would have done without you."

Gray wanted to argue her own guilt further, but she realized that wouldn't help Savannah. "Come on, let's get you home. A hot shower and a cup of tea will work wonders for you."

Savannah did indeed look better after a shower, curled up on the couch with a mug of tea cradled between her palms. "Come sit with me, Gray."

Gray did so, and Savannah immediately pushed herself into Gray's arms. If it had been any other day, Gray would have politely extracted herself, refusing to cooperate with Savannah's continued attempts of seduction. This was no seduction, though. This was simply Savannah looking for comfort and wanting to feel safe.

So, Gray pulled Savannah close to her chest, running a hand through her hair. "You're alright. I'm going to keep you safe; I promise. I'm assigning someone else to your case tomorrow—someone who won't make the same mistake I did."

"What?" The mug of tea went tumbling to the floor. "Gray, no! You can't leave me. Please, I need you."

"You need someone who isn't emotionally

involved, who can put the job ahead of their feelings. That's not me, not anymore."

"I don't care. I want you. I'm not accepting anyone else."

"Why must you be so infuriating?" Gray murmured, stroking Savannah's hair gently. "Don't you see that this is for the best?"

"I want *you*, Gray. I need you to stay."

Gray couldn't deny her anything. "Very well."

She would have to do a better job of distancing herself from Savannah emotionally; today had shown that much. It was probably inadvisable, but she couldn't bring herself to abandon Savannah when Savannah was asking her to stay.

They turned on some mindless sitcom and watched in silence, both absorbed in their own thoughts. Savannah eventually drifted off in Gray's arms. Gray was struck by how right it felt, holding Savannah like this.

Savannah woke with a start about an hour later.

"You're okay," Gray murmured. "You're safe."

Savannah sighed and relaxed, tipping her head back so that she could look at Gray. "Well, hello there. You look comfortable." She batted her eyelashes and wriggled her body against Gray's, her ass digging tantalizingly into Gray's groin. Gray did her best not to moan. So, seductive Savannah was back. She must be feeling better.

Gray carefully extracted herself from Savannah's embrace and got up off the couch. "We'll need to follow up with the police station. Touching base with the initial guys on the scene wasn't enough. The sooner they can start investigating, the better. In the meantime, you should stay at home until they make some progress on tracking down your would-be kidnappers."

"No way. I'm not going to stop living my life. If I do that, then they've already won."

"They haven't won until they have you in their clutches, and I'm trying to make sure that doesn't happen. You need to listen to me for once, Savannah, and stay put."

"I'll be fine. I have you to protect me."

"That's just what I'm telling you," Gray said through gritted teeth. "I can't guarantee that I can protect you if you keep putting yourself in risky situations. It's just too dangerous for you to be going about your normal life right now."

"It'll be fine," Savannah said airily. Gray wished that Savannah would take her own safety more seriously.

She'd have to figure out a way to keep Savannah in the house. Maybe she could start getting more of Savannah's friends over for pool parties or something like that.

As annoyed as she was, that annoyance was tinged with fondness, and that just made Gray even more irritated. What was it about Savannah that allowed her to get under Gray's skin like this?

She's my client, Gray reminded herself. If she wanted to keep Savannah safe, she had better get that into the forefront of her mind and keep it there. If something happened to Savannah because Gray had failed to protect her, Gray knew that she'd never forgive herself.

9

SAVANNAH

Savannah closed her eyes, trying to lose herself in the kiss. Ruth was beautiful and athletic. Savannah was sure that she'd be a great lover... and yet, Savannah just wasn't feeling it. An image of Gray's face kept popping up in her head, which was distracting, to say the least.

She pulled away. "I'm sorry, Ruth. I guess I'm just not in the mood tonight."

"I bet I could get you in the mood." Ruth's hand strayed toward Savannah's panties, an invitation that Savannah wouldn't usually be able to resist, but right now, all she wanted was to flop down on Gray's bed and chat with her until they were both too tired to keep their eyes open anymore.

"Maybe next time. Can I walk you out?"

Ruth made a noise of disappointment but took the rejection gracefully. Savannah kissed her once more on the doorstep before regretfully sending her away. She hurried to Gray's room, already eager to see her, even though she had seen her less than two hours ago.

Gray was sitting at the desk in her room, going over some boring papers the police had sent. Savannah pranced in and lay down on Gray's bed, letting her head tilt over the edge of the bed and looking at Gray upside down.

"How's it going?"

Gray put the papers aside and turned to her. "I'm almost finished going through the police reports. Your father was very helpful in pulling some strings to allow me access to their investigation. But what are you doing here? I wasn't expecting to see you again until morning."

Gray didn't sound entirely surprised. It wasn't the first time in recent days that Savannah had sent a date home early to come and talk to her.

Savannah shrugged. "We just didn't connect."

It was hard to feel a connection to anyone when her connection to Gray overshadowed what seemed like pale comparisons.

Gray smiled and came to lie down beside

Savannah on the bed, both of them facing the canopy above. "How is that painting going? The one of the sunflower?"

"I think I'm getting there. That idea we found online for the texturing is really helping. I'm hoping that I can finish it in the next few days."

"It's going to be spectacular when it's done. I mean, it's already spectacular and it's only half-finished. I can't wait to see it when it's finished."

Maybe Savannah would give it to Gray. She'd given Gray a lot of paintings recently. It was getting a bit ridiculous, but Gray was so happy every time Savannah presented her with a new one. They had even made several trips to Gray's apartment to put them up, deciding together where the best spots for them would be.

Savannah was still doing her modeling, much to Gray's frustration. She understood Gray's point —she definitely didn't want to be kidnapped, but Savannah had a good point, too. She didn't want to put her life on hold for what could be months, or even years, while the police and Gray worked to catch those responsible for the threat to her safety.

She had cut down on shopping and restaurant trips, but still went clubbing occasionally with her friends. This made Gray so grumpy that Savannah more often than not invited her friends over to her house for a pool party or an evening of drinks.

Gray insisted that this wasn't really her scene and hovered in the background. After everyone was gone, Savannah would drop the attitude she kept up with Gray in public and talk to her more openly. More than once, she sent her friends home early simply to have more time to spend with Gray before bedtime.

Savannah hadn't forgotten her goal of finally seducing Gray. She seemed to want Gray more and more with every passing day. It wasn't even just about the sex anymore. Savannah wanted to be with Gray more intimately, to know her from the inside out. She wanted to be the reason Gray moaned in pleasure and lost control.

Days later, Savannah was working on her flower paintings again, but today, there was a different painting in her head. She didn't have anything else planned, so she was spending the entire day in her studio, something she had always wanted to do but hadn't felt right doing.

Gray had encouraged her to do what she

wanted, regardless of what other people might think, so here she was, staring at a blank canvas, wondering if she could pull off the image in her head. Well, she wouldn't know unless she tried. At worst, she'd toss the failed painting away and go back to her flowers.

Gray was on the opposite side of the canvas, unable to see what Savannah was painting, as she knew that Savannah liked privacy while she did her work. She was happy to share the painting afterward, but while she created it, she liked it to be hers alone.

Savannah glanced at Gray, though she hardly needed to. She knew Gray's face so well by now that she could probably paint it with her eyes shut.

Several hours later, Savannah surveyed her painting in satisfaction. It showed her and Gray lying on Savannah's bed, facing each other in relaxed postures with smiles on their faces. It was exactly how Savannah imagined they must look during their late-night talks.

"Gray, I'm done. Come and look at this."

Gray hurried around to Savannah's side of the canvas, her expression eager. Savannah loved how enthusiastic Gray always was about seeing her paintings.

Gray's mouth fell open as she took in the painting. "Savannah... it's beautiful."

Gray was right. It was one of Savannah's best works. "I was feeling inspired. It's for you," Savannah said shyly.

Now Gray was staring at her with an expression of wonder. Her eyes flicked down to Savannah's lips.

Savannah saw her chance and stepped forward, wrapping her arms around Gray and kissing her.

Gray moaned into Savannah's mouth, and that moan sounded like a surrender and a promise all in one.

They kissed fiercely, Gray's hands digging into Savannah's hips as she took control of the kiss, plundering Savannah's mouth.

Savannah felt her back slamming up against the wall, knocking the breath out of her, but Gray was already breathing new air into her lungs with the kiss that never ended.

Savannah wrapped first one leg and then the other around Gray's waist. Gray easily took her weight and carried Savannah through to the bedroom, never breaking the kiss.

Gray threw Savannah down onto the bed and

pounced. She ripped Savannah's shirt open, sending buttons flying everywhere.

"You have no idea how long I've wanted to do this," Gray growled. Fuck, she was so sexy like this.

"I'm yours," Savannah breathed. She wanted Gray to have her wicked way with her. She wanted to be taken so thoroughly that she wouldn't be able to think of other women ever after this. Her body was crying out for Gray, and Gray finally seemed willing to give Savannah what she had wanted for weeks now.

Savannah tried to wriggle out of her pants, but Gray beat her to it, ripping the pants open, exposing Savannah's underwear. That went quickly too, leaving Savannah naked before her. Savannah reached up to touch Gray, but Gray slapped her hands away, moving them to the headboard.

"Hold here and don't let go."

A shiver of desire went through Savannah's body as she did as Gray said, clutching the headboard tightly in both hands. Gray started sucking wet kisses to Savannah's neck, hard enough to leave bruises.

Savannah should probably tell her to stop. It

was going to be hell to cover these with makeup for her next modeling shoot.

She didn't want Gray to stop, though. She was so turned on that she was practically coming out of her skin with desire. Her pussy was soaked already and her clit was throbbing angrily, demanding attention. Savannah clenched her legs together, trying to give herself some relief, but all that did was frustrate her even further.

Gray finally made her way down to Savannah's breasts. She sucked hard on first one nipple then the other.

"Gray," Savannah whined. "Please, I need more."

"You're demanding, aren't you?" Gray murmured. "Very well—you asked for it."

She thrust three fingers deep into Savannah's pussy. Savannah cried out and arched into the touch. Gray was already moving her fingers in and out at a brutal pace. Savannah liked it rough and she knew that Gray had seen her in action enough to know this. Gray was giving her exactly what she wanted. Savannah rocked her hips to meet Gray's movements, her pussy clenching around the delicious intrusion.

Gray moved back to Savannah's nipples, licking

around them before finally pulling one into her mouth again.

Her fingers inside Savannah were rough and demanding and so utterly perfect that Savannah thought she might come just like this.

Savannah clutched the headboard as Gray's mouth slowly moved down, kissing her stomach and finally brushing over the blonde curls above her pussy.

Savannah gasped as Gray's tongue flicked over her clit. Gray did it again, quickly setting up a rhythm in time with her thrusts.

"Gray, I'm not going to last. Fuck, I'm so close."

Gray made no answer except to double down, licking and sucking on Savannah's clit as her fingers continued to work deep inside Savannah.

Savannah's back arched and she screamed as she came harder than she ever had in her life, convulsing on Gray's fingers, clutching at the head-board for dear life.

Gray kept going until Savannah was limp and wrung out, whimpering slightly at the oversensitivity.

When Gray pulled back, her eyes were dark with desire.

Savannah let go of the headboard and reached

for her, but Gray once more slapped her hands aside. "Did I say you could let go?"

"But don't you want—?"

"I want you to watch as I get myself off."

Savannah pouted. She wanted to touch Gray, but Gray clearly wasn't having any of it. Still, she couldn't deny the lure of watching Gray touch herself, so she nodded.

Gray lay back and pushed a hand into her pants. Savannah could see from the movements that Gray was working her clit every bit as hard as she had worked Savannah's.

It didn't take long. Gray let out a strangled cry as she came, and Savannah saw her pants darkening with wetness. She smiled as Gray wriggled out of them.

"Take your shirt off," Savannah urged, and Gray sighed but acquiesced and pulled her shirt and her sports bra over her head.

Then she pulled Savannah into her arms. Savannah snuggled eagerly, feeling Gray's small breasts pressing against her. She wished Gray had allowed her to touch, but she was hardly in the mood to complain while still recovering from the best orgasm she'd ever had.

"This can't be more than sex," Gray said

quietly, stroking Savannah's arm. "You're still my client. I can't get emotionally involved. It's my emotional involvement that allowed your attackers to escape before."

Savannah did her best to hide her disappointment. She was usually all for casual sex, but she knew that with Gray, she was falling in love with her.

Gray apparently didn't feel the same. Or wouldn't allow herself to at least. Savannah wondered if things would be different once Gray had successfully removed the threat. Once Savannah was no longer her client, would Gray be open to more?

For now, Savannah knew that she would have to play by Gray's rules, but there was no reason she couldn't lay the groundwork for something more in the future. She had successfully seduced Gray into her bed. Now, she would seduce Gray into her heart.

"Of course," she said easily. Let Gray think that she was happy with casual sex—it certainly wouldn't be a stretch of the imagination.

Gray seemed satisfied and kissed the back of Savannah's neck. Savannah sighed happily, relaxing in Gray's arms as she plotted. Gray had told her about Amelia. Savannah knew that sleeping with her was a big deal for Gray. She hadn't done it with anyone else since Amelia had died.

Gray would no doubt have feelings she needed to work through. Savannah needed to take things slow and not scare her away. She wanted to be in this for the long haul, not just a few good rounds. For this to work, she'd need to handle it delicately and give Gray time to work through the guilt she was no doubt feeling.

Sooner or later, she would win Gray's heart. She would make sure of it.

10

GRAY

ray's eyes flew open. She realized that she and Savannah must have drifted off. It wasn't entirely surprising. The sex had been intense, and it was so comfortable here in Savannah's bed, with Savannah sleeping peacefully in her arms.

Gray carefully extracted herself and went to check on the cameras. Once she was sure that everything was safe, she leaned back in the chair in the surveillance room, thinking. She had never meant to give in to Savannah, but now that she had, she couldn't find it in herself to regret it.

The sex had been incredible, but the act of being close to Savannah had been just as alluring. That was the part Gray was worried about. Meaningless sex was one thing. Getting feelings involved was a whole other mess.

Gray simply had to make sure that it remained just sex. Even in her most optimistic imaginings, she didn't envision herself ensuring it didn't happen again. She was only human, after all, and she didn't have the self-control to turn down Savannah.

She hadn't even let Savannah touch her, and it had been the best sex she'd ever had. Watching Savannah fall apart under her touch like that had turned Gray on so much that she'd felt like she was about to explode out of her skin.

Gray wondered if she should let Savannah touch her next time. She couldn't deny the allure of the idea. She could guide Savannah on just how best to touch her, losing herself in the pleasure of Savannah's fingers and tongue.

The thought was enough for Gray's body to wake up fully and take interest. She rolled her eyes. Before Savannah, it had been years before she felt any kind of sexual desire toward anyone else. Now, her body seemed determined to act like a horny teenager.

Gray returned to the bedroom, where Savannah was still sleeping peacefully. She should take up a guard position outside the door. It would be the right thing to do—the professional thing to do.

As much as Gray told herself to go stand outside the door, she somehow found herself slipping back into bed with Savannah. Savannah mumbled something under her breath and turned so that she was in Gray's arms. Gray couldn't help grinning. This was perfect.

She forced herself to stay awake and alert for any threat as Savannah made the most adorable noises in her sleep. Gray spent her time memorizing Savannah's face, wondering when she'd next get the opportunity to be so close to her.

Savannah seemed to tire of partners quickly. Maybe she wouldn't want Gray anymore, now that she had succeeded in her goal of seducing her. Gray hoped not.

Savannah woke about an hour later. She stretched, looking up at Gray before letting her eyes drop shyly to the mattress. "Hi."

"Hi." Gray wondered what else she should say. There were a few moments of awkward silence before Savannah spoke. "We should go to lunch."

"Yeah, we should do that."

They walked in silence to lunch, probably both

wondering what to say. Gray wasn't sure how to approach this change in their dynamic. Savannah clearly wasn't, either. Gray was a little surprised that Savannah seemed as wrong-footed as she was.

After all, Savannah was no stranger to casual sex. It was Gray who was the complete beginner in this regard. She had every reason to feel uncertain and awkward, but she didn't know why Savannah would be feeling the same.

"I want to get my nails done."

"It's a bad idea," Gray said at once. "Too risky."

"But Gray," Savannah whined. "Look at them." She held out her perfectly manicured nails.

Gray rolled her eyes, a habit she was quickly picking up from Savannah. "Your nails will survive, Savannah." A thought struck her. She gave Savannah what she hoped was a flirty smile. "Besides, I can think of better things to do with our time." Two could play at this seduction game.

Savannah caught onto her meaning at once. "I like the way you're thinking."

She pushed aside the remains of her meal and came to straddle Gray. Gray leaned in and kissed her, hard and fast and urgent.

Savannah kissed back just as fiercely. Gray stood and brushed aside the plates, sending them flying and slamming Savannah's back onto the table. Savannah moaned loudly and squirmed but didn't try to get away.

Gray pulled Savannah's pants roughly down, exposing her wetness. She spread Savannah's folds and dove in, licking her firmly from bottom to top. Savannah squealed and writhed under her. Gray pressed her hands to Savannah's hips, preventing her from moving.

Gray was well aware that someone could walk in on them at any moment, but that only added to the appeal of their current position. She moved further down, pushing her tongue inside Savannah to taste her before moving back up to her clit. Savannah was soaked and crying out on Gray's tongue, her hands clenching and unclenching convulsively at her sides.

"Gray, I'm going to—"

Savannah didn't get a chance to finish her sentence as her orgasm overtook her. She squirted all over the table and Gray's chin as she came, her cry echoing around the dining room. Gray kept licking her until she was sure that she had wrung every last ounce of pleasure from the orgasm. She smiled to herself. Savannah was so fucking beautiful. Giving her pleasure was the most exquisite thing in the world.

Then she took Savanna's hand, pulling her to her feet, where Savannah stood wobbling slightly.

"Come on. We're going to the bedroom, and then I'm going to sit on your face. You're going to take it quietly like a good girl. You're going to lick me just the way I want you to, until I come on your pretty little face. Do you like the sound of that?"

"Fuck, yes," Savannah breathed. She scurried to the bedroom ahead of Gray, lying down on the bed and gesturing impatiently. "Come on, then."

Gray grinned as she took her pants off and swung one leg over the side of Savannah's face. Savannah started licking her eagerly at once. Gray ground her hips down onto Savanna's face, forcing Savannah's tongue more firmly against her clit.

It felt so good, so much better than touching herself. Gray didn't know how she'd survived this long without sex. Now that she was reacquainted with how good it was, she didn't think she'd ever be letting Savannah out of bed.

She rode Savannah's face at a brutal pace, but Savannah made no noise of protest. Her hands were on Gray's hips, encouraging her rocking, and her tongue was doing such delicious things that Gray felt herself swiftly hurtling toward the edge.

She pushed herself forward, urging Savannah's tongue just slightly higher on her clit. She hit the perfect spot, and it was too much for Gray. Gray screamed as she came on Savannah's face, jerking her hips back and forth as she rode out her orgasm until it faded away in a rush of heat.

She collapsed inelegantly to the side. Savannah chuckled and folded herself into Gray's arms. Gray eagerly pulled Savannah close. "I'm not letting you out of this bed today," she growled, putting a possessive hand on one of Savannah's breasts. "Probably not tomorrow, either."

"I can live with that." Savannah's voice was breathy and already laced with desire. Gray wondered how long before they were both recovered enough to go again. She was already imagining all the wicked things she could do to Savannah, things she hadn't thought about since Amelia.

Amelia...

"Are you alright?"

Gray sighed. "Yes. I'm just thinking."

"About Amelia?" Savannah guessed.

Gray propped herself up on one elbow to look at Savannah. "How did you know that?"

"You looked sad. It's okay, you know. You told me that she'd want you to move on after mourning for her. I'm sure she wouldn't begrudge you some hot sex."

That had Gray chuckling. "No, she wouldn't. She'd probably be horrified by how long I went without it, actually."

"Well, I guess we'll just need to make up for lost time." Savannah crawled up so that she was straddling Gray and kissed her.

Gray moaned and kissed Savannah back. "I can live with that."

She reflected that she'd finally found a way to keep Savannah home and safe. Maybe she wasn't being as unprofessional as she had originally thought. After all, if sex was the only thing that would keep Savannah from endangering her life, then if you thought about it, it was really Gray's duty to give her orgasm after orgasm until they were both too tired to come any more.

And if it was a pleasant duty, so much the better.

"Gray, come on," Savannah whined. "My nails have never looked so disgusting in my life."

Gray glanced at Savannah's nails. They weren't as perfect as they usually were, but there was certainly nothing wrong with them. "How about I do them for you?"

Savannah raised an eyebrow. "Do you know how to do nails?"

"I'm a quick learner."

"No way. I am not about to be your guinea pig. We can go to that little out-of-the-way place we went to last time. It'll be safe enough."

"The police still haven't caught the people responsible, but the threat is still out there, and Herom is losing more and more money every day. Every day they don't have you is a day their business suffers. They must be growing more and more desperate. I worry that even a small out-of-the-way place won't be safe."

Savannah folded her arms. "Well, then you'll just have to protect me. I want my nails done, and that's final."

So, Savannah the brat was back. Maybe Gray could bring back Savannah the seductress. "I bet I could change your mind," she purred, leaning in close and kissing the shell of Savannah's ear. She gripped Savanna's ass with one hand and caressed a breast with the other. "How about I take you back to the bedroom and see just how loudly I can make you scream?"

Savannah moaned softly, and for a moment, Gray thought she had won, but then Savannah straightened, pulling out of her grip. "No, Gray. We can do that later. Right now, I'm going to the nail bar. You may accompany me or stay here, but I'm leaving."

Gray growled under her breath, but followed Savannah, muttering about difficult clients and multiple attack points.

Savannah tried to convince Gray to get her nails done too, but Gray insisted on staying on her feet, keeping a sharp lookout. If anyone came here, she was going to be ready for them.

The appointment seemed to take forever. Savannah sighed happily as her nails were tended to. Well, at least one of them was happy. Gray just hoped that Savannah was right and nothing would happen. However, she hadn't gotten to be this good at her job by not being paranoid. She had to assume the worst, because all too often, the worst was what she got.

Gray was just starting to think that perhaps

this whole thing would go off without a hitch when she spotted them. At least ten men, all headed toward the small nail salon. All of them were carrying automatic weapons.

"Savannah, we have to go."

"But my nails are almost—"

"*Now!*"

Gray grabbed Savannah's wrist, yanking it and causing the nail technician's brush to streak across her hand. Savannah's indignant noise died in her throat when she saw what Gray was looking at. She squeaked in alarm and hide herself behind Gray but hiding would do them no good. They had to escape.

"Is there a back entrance?" Gray demanded.

The nail technician shook her head, staring with wide eyes at the quickly approaching men.

"Right, I'm going to cause a distraction. As soon as I break a hole in their line, you need to run through, Savannah, got it?"

"But they'll shoot you."

"They'll be reluctant to shoot. It could draw police attention to the area before they successfully escape with you, which gives us a small advantage."

"I don't want to leave you behind!"

"Savannah, this is no time to argue! Do as I say! Please, trust me. I'm here to protect you. That's my job."

"I don't—"

They were out of time. Gray grabbed a chair and opened the door, throwing the chair directly into the line of advancing men. They scattered to avoid it and Gray dove for the nearest one, tackling him to the ground. "Now, Savannah!"

For a terrible moment, she feared that Savannah wouldn't follow her instructions, but then Savannah streaked by, aiming for the gap in the men that Gray had created.

It wasn't enough. Gray quickly knocked out the man under her with a blow to the back of the head, but the man on her other side managed to grab Savannah around the waist. Savannah screamed and tried to kick him, but he quickly controlled her arms and legs.

Gray leaped up and wrapped an arm around his neck, choking him. He let go of Savannah to try to undo her hold, but there were already two more men grabbing Savannah, and three coming at Gray from behind. There were just too many of them.

Gray elbowed one in the face and stamped on the instep of another. It wasn't enough. Her arms were grabbed and her legs were controlled next. Savannah was screaming and fighting, but she had no strength to match these men.

Gray was supposed to be her strength, and Gray was failing her. Seeing Savannah in such a state of terror filled Gray with a fury she had seldom felt before. How dare these men harm her sweet, innocent Savannah? Gray would make them pay for it.

She roared with the effort as she managed to break free, hitting one man in the face hard enough to drop him into an unmoving pile of limbs on the ground. She kicked another in the groin and he went down too.

Gray knew that her advantage was going to run out. Sooner or later—probably sooner—these men would decide that she was too much trouble to keep alive and just shoot her, taking the risk of summoning the police. It was Savannah they needed alive, after all. Gray was dispensable.

She had to disable them before that happened, but there were four still standing. One of them tackled Gray to the ground. She twisted out from under him, only to have another one throw himself on top of her. Gray kneed him in the stomach, knocking the wind out of him, but one of his companions grabbed her by the collar.

Her hands were trapped and she could do nothing when she saw the butt of the gun coming straight toward her temple.

There was a blinding flash of pain and everything went black.

11

SAVANNAH

"Gray! *Gray!*" Savannah screamed in panic. Had they killed her? Was she still breathing? Savannah couldn't tell. The thought of something happening to Gray sent pain ripping through her insides. It was unacceptable. She couldn't allow it to happen.

One of the men pulled out a knife, bringing it up to Gray's throat.

"My father will pay for her!" That gave the men pause. "He'll pay you good money for her safe return," Savannah quickly continued. "She's a dear family friend. He'll do anything to ensure her safety."

"What do you think, Erik?"

Erik, who seemed to be the leader, nodded

slowly. "I don't see any harm in getting ourselves a little bonus. He'll have the girl; that's all he wants. We can keep the guard and ransom her off to the father for cash while he does his negotiations for whatever he wants from her father."

Savannah could have collapsed in relief. She only hoped that her father would indeed pay for Gray. Surely, he wouldn't let her die, not just for money. Besides, Gray was Savannah's only chance of getting out of this. Simon must know that. If he wanted Savannah to escape without having to give in to her kidnappers' demands, he needed to keep Gray alive so that she could orchestrate that escape.

Savannah wondered dismally what her father would choose, if it really came down to it—her or his business. He would try to have it both ways, of course, but if he truly had to make a choice, Savannah wasn't certain that he'd pick her. She knew he loved her, in his way, but money had always been his first love.

Savannah and Gray were bundled into a van. Savannah scrambled over to Gray, pulling Gray's head into her lap. She was still breathing, and Savannah could feel a steady pulse. She would have collapsed in relief if she wasn't worried about squashing Gray with her body weight.

Not that Gray seemed to mind Savannah being on top of her. Savannah remembered the last time she had sat on Gray's face, riding her tongue to an explosive orgasm that took her breath away. She felt herself blushing and glanced at her captors, as if they could tell what she was thinking just by the shade of her cheeks.

Now was not the time for sexy thoughts. Savannah tried to think what Gray would do in this situation. No doubt something smart and competent that would lead to them escaping, but Savannah couldn't think of anything to do but wait for Gray to wake up and do her best to follow whatever plan Gray came up with.

Gray had been right all along. Why had Savannah had to get her stupid nails done? Now they could both die, all for a manicure. If they ever got out of this, she resolved to be less materialistic and shallow about appearances.

If they got out of this.

They were taken to a warehouse and tied up. Savannah tried to loosen the ropes around her wrists, but the attempt only made them pull tighter, so she stopped. One of the men—Justin, she heard Erik call him—stayed to guard them while the others left, presumably to do whatever they did when not kidnapping people.

"You know, you can make a lot of money from me. Whatever you're being paid, my father will pay double for my safe return."

That much, Savannah knew to be true. Simon wouldn't have a problem paying a ransom. He certainly had the cash for it. What he might not be willing to do is change his business practices in a way that would be less profitable, as that would affect the accumulation of his future fortune, as if he needed more money.

It was in her best interest to negotiate with these men before she was handed off to Herom.

"Shut your mouth, or I'll gag you."

"You have no idea how rich you could be," Savannah coaxed. "I could—"

Justin got out a roll of duct tape and stalked over to her.

"Okay, okay, I'm sorry! I'll keep quiet now."

"You'd better."

He walked off, leaving Savannah at a loss for what to do. She was just contemplating how screwed she was when Gray groaned and opened her eyes.

"Gray!" Savannah kept her voice at a whisper, hoping that Justin wouldn't hear and tape her mouth shut. "Are you okay? How are you feeling?"

"I've felt worse," Gray said grimly. She looked around the room. "How long was I out for?"

"Not long—maybe half an hour."

"Good. We need to get out of here before we're handed over to Herom."

"I know, but I can't figure out how. I've already tried bribery, but I was turned down, and I don't have anything else in my arsenal."

"I do." Gray gave her a reassuring smile before turning to Justin. "Hey, you! I need to piss."

"Hold it," Justin snapped.

"I've been holding it for hours while this one insisted on getting her nails all prettied up. Now, unless you want me to piss myself, I suggest you find me a bathroom."

"Fine," Justin grumbled. "Just don't cause any trouble."

"I just want a toilet. That's all."

Justin pulled Gray to her feet.

"You'll need to untie me, unless you want to pull down my pants and wipe for me."

He sneered at her. "Yeah, I am so not doing that. I'll have my gun on you the whole time, you understand? I don't care how much you're worth, if you look like you're even thinking of causing trouble, I'm putting a bullet in your head. Understand?"

"Perfectly. Let's hurry this up, shall we? I really do need to go."

"Yeah, yeah, I heard you the first time."

Justin untied Gray and reached for his gun, no doubt to hold her at gunpoint while he took her to the bathroom.

Gray never gave him the chance. She grabbed his wrist, yanking sharply down and bringing her knee up into his face. She brought an elbow down right on the back of his skull and Justin dropped like a stone.

Hope leaped in Savannah's stomach. Maybe they could get out of this after all.

"Come on." Gray used Justin's knife to cut Savannah's ropes and the two of them headed for the door, Gray holding Justin's gun.

The door didn't lead to the outside, but to a corridor. There was no choice of routes, so Gray and Savannah hurried down the corridor as quietly as they could.

At the end of the corridor was another door.

"Stay back," Gray breathed. "I'll check it out."

Before she could do more than take a few steps toward the door, it opened.

"It's about time for me to relieve Justin. I hope they haven't been causing him any—hey!"

Erik drew his gun, but it was too late. Gray shot him in the head. Unfortunately, it seemed that the rest of the crew was with Erik, and at the sound of the shot, they all came bursting into the corridor.

"Savannah, get down!" Gray shouted.

Savannah dropped to the floor, covering her head with her hands as gunshots rang out. She saw Gray dive behind a wooden crate and fire shots from behind it. One man was hit in the shoulder. He bashed his head on the wall going down and was knocked out. Another, she got in the chest. Two more in the head.

There were only three standing now, but one of them was creeping around the crate that Gray was hiding behind.

Gray shot the last two men—how had Savannah not known she was such a good shot?—but the last was coming up behind her.

"Gray, watch out!"

Gray turned and straightened up, which meant the shot aimed at her head instead went into her stomach. Savannah screamed as Gray stumbled back. Gray's aim wavered for a moment, but then she steadied and hit him in the head.

Savannah scrambled over to Gray's side as Gray sank to her knees, clutching at her stomach.

"Gray!"

"I'm okay, Savannah. It didn't hit anything vital —it just hurts. I'll be fine as long as I get medical attention."

"Medical attention. Right."

Savannah dug through the pockets of their fallen kidnappers until she found a cellphone.

She made the 911 call, probably coming off as completely hysterical, but she didn't care. It didn't matter if they understood her or not. They would track the call here regardless. She tossed the phone aside and went back to Gray's side.

Savannah pressed her hands over Gray's, putting pressure on the wound. Gray said it hadn't hit anything vital, but this was a lot of blood.

"Shh, I'll be okay," Gray soothed.

Savannah gave a choked laugh. Gray had just been shot, and she was trying to comfort Savannah. "I should be the one trying to make you feel better."

Gray shrugged. "I've been through much worse

than this. You haven't. Don't worry, you're safe now."

Her eyes fluttered.

"No, Gray, stay with me!"

"I'll be fine, Savannah. It's just the blood loss. The doctors will fix me right up."

"No, Gray, you have to stay awake!"

Too late. Gray's eyes rolled up in her head as she passed out.

The wait was excruciating. It seemed to take forever, but Savannah finally heard the sound of sirens in the distance. When they got close, she started yelling, drawing the paramedics to her. Gray was loaded into the ambulance, and of course, Savannah went with her.

When they got to the hospital, Gray was rushed into surgery.

"Please, will she be okay?" Savannah asked the doctor tearfully.

"Are you family?"

"Yes," Savannah said without thinking. "Yes, she's my family."

He gave her a reassuring smile. "She should be fine. She's lost a lot of blood, but we're putting her on an infusion now. There's no reason to think she won't pull through. The bullet doesn't seem to have hit anything vital."

"Thank you. Thank you." Savannah clasped the doctor's hand briefly before letting him go tend to Gray.

One of the nurses kindly offered her some scrubs and a chance to shower. Savannah was covered in Gray's blood, and she took the opportunity eagerly. She couldn't believe that just a few hours before, she had been worried about the state of her nails.

The police wanted her to come down to the station, but she insisted that she wanted to be here when Gray woke up, so they agreed to question her in the hospital waiting room.

Simon came to assure himself that Savanah was okay, and to make sure that the police were doing everything they could to catch whoever those men were working for. They were questioning the one man who had survived—the one who knocked his head as he fell—and Simon seemed confident that they would cut a deal with him that would lead right to Herom.

The people within Herom responsible for this would be arrested, and the threat to Savannah would be removed. She should be pleased, but all she felt was a gnawing worry for Gray. The doctors thought it would be okay, but unexpected things happened in surgery all the time.

Of course, watching *Grey's Anatomy* hardly made her an expert on surgery, but she knew enough to know that medical procedures didn't always go as planned. What if something went wrong? She would never be able to live with herself if Gray died because Savannah had wanted to get her stupid nails done.

She didn't want to live without Gray in her life.

The realization hit Savannah as suddenly as things had gone badly at that nail bar.

She didn't want to keep going without Gray.

As much as she had tried to respect Gray's wish to keep things between them casual, she had failed. No matter how much she had denied it to herself before, Savannah couldn't deny it anymore. She needed Gray.

She was in love with Gray.

She'd never been in love before, and hadn't even known she knew what it felt like, but now, having nearly lost the woman who had somehow come to mean more to her than anyone else in the world, she *knew*. This was what love was.

Did Gray feel the same, underneath all her

professionalism? Or did she still see Savannah as nothing more than an irritating client with a great body?

There was only one way to find out.

Savannah leaped up the moment she saw the doctor. "Is she okay? Is she awake?"

"She's fine. She's asleep for now, but you can see her, if you like. She's in recovery, room twenty-three."

The doctor kept speaking, but Savannah wasn't listening. She was rushing toward room twenty-three, bursting through the door and hurrying to Gray's bedside.

As the doctor had said, Gray was asleep. Savannah pulled up a chair and gently took Gray's hand. She would wait for however long it took.

It took two hours, but finally, Gray's eyes fluttered open.

"Savannah?" she mumbled.

Savannah squeezed her hand. "I'm here, my love."

Gray's eyes became more alert. "Are you alright? You're not hurt, are you?"

"I'm fine, now that you're awake. I was so worried for you."

Gray's gaze softened. "I told you I'd be okay."

Savannah pressed a kiss to the back of Gray's hand. "Gray, I love you."

Gray's eyes widened. Savannah waited with anticipation, but she wasn't left to wait long. "I love you too, Savannah. I don't know how, but somehow, I've fallen for you. I guess there goes my record for professionalism."

Savannah laughed and leaned in, pressing a chaste kiss to Gray's lips. "I can't believe you love me too. Aren't I just an annoying rich brat?"

"Sure, but you're my annoying rich brat. I wouldn't have you any other way."

That had her laughing again. "I promise, I'll try to be better. I'm going to give up modeling. That whole industry is too focused on appearance and possessions anyway. I'm going to have your guy look at my paintings and try to make a living from that. I'm sick of being under my father's control."

Gray's gaze warmed her from the inside. "I'm so proud of you, Savannah. I'll be here to support you if your father pulls funding while you're still finding your feet when it comes to your painting career."

"You don't have to—"

"I want to. I'm not sure if you're aware, but your

father paid me a rather ridiculous amount of money to guard you. Trust me, I'm doing fine. My business is doing well. I can support both of us for a time."

Savannah didn't like the idea of relying on Gray for money, but it meant the world to her that Gray was willing to stick her neck out to support Savannah's painting. Savannah would try to ensure that her father didn't find out about her change of plans until it was too late for him to deny her access to her trust fund, leaving her with nothing until she got on her feet.

Either way, it was something for her and Gray to figure out, together.

"Move in with me."

Gray raised an eyebrow. "Moving a bit fast, aren't we? Don't you want to go on a real date first?"

"I know what I want, Gray. I want you. Move in with me?"

Gray's expression melted into a helpless smile. "I never could refuse you anything. Of course I'll move in with you."

There would be hurdles to leap, but Savanah was certain that she could make it with Gray at her side. She felt strong with Gray, as if Gray's competence and capability rubbed off on her just by being in her vicinity.

Gray squeezed Savannah's hand and smiled, and as Savannah smiled back, she knew that everything was right with the world.

EPILOGUE

"Gray," Savannah whined. "It's late."

"I know, my love. I'm almost done with this paperwork. Ten more minutes, I promise."

Savannah pouted but didn't argue further. She knew how important Gray's work was to her.

It had been a big decision, choosing to take a step back from personal guarding and move to managing her business from behind a desk. Gray still missed it sometimes, but mostly, she was glad just to be able to spend more time with Savannah.

Previously she had been happy to give up what little there was of her own life to live a client's life 24/7, but now she had Savannah, she no longer was prepared to sacrifice her own life for a client.

For her part, Savannah's painting business was booming. Simon was practically apoplectic with rage that he no longer had any means with which to control her, but there was nothing he could do about it. He had frozen her trust fund, but the house was already in her name, and she and Gray made plenty of money together, enough to afford them a comfortable lifestyle, if not quite as extravagant as what Savannah had been used to before.

Savannah was a changed woman from the bratty rich girl Gray had first encountered. She was more thoughtful and less materialistic. She made more of an effort to listen to Gray, even when what Gray had to say wasn't what she wanted to hear.

They were two very different people, and it wasn't always easy, but Gray never doubted for a moment that it was worth it.

Gray finished answering the last of her client emails and shut down her laptop. She turned to find that Savannah had changed into lingerie and was spread out on the bed in a seductive pose.

"Are you sure I can't tempt you away from work?" she purred.

If Gray hadn't already been finished with work, this certainly would have tested her resolve.

She pretended to think about it, just to get under Savannah's skin. "Well, I still have a few more phone calls to make, which are kind of important..."

"Or you could get out your strap-on and see just how loudly you can make me scream."

How Savannah could get Gray wet with nothing more than words was something that Gray would never understand.

She gave up all pretense and pounced, pinning Savannah to the bed. Savannah pretended to struggle against the grip, but Gray knew that she loved it. She held Savannah down and kissed her thoroughly. Savannah moaned and arched up into the kiss.

Gray wanted to rip that sexy lingerie right off her, but Savannah had reprimanded her about ruining too many of her clothes, so Gray needed to be careful. She flipped Savannah over onto her stomach to undo her bra strap, then pulled her panties down her hips to her ankles.

Gray grabbed Savannah's hips and pulled them upward, maneuvering her onto her hands and knees.

"Spread your legs."

Savannah did so and Gray immediately pushed a finger inside her. Savannah was, as usual, already wet and ready for her. Gray started pumping in and out of her, enjoying the feeling of Savannah clenching around her.

"Gray, I need more."

"Whiny today, aren't you?"

"You love it."

Gray could practically feel Savannah's smirk. "I do," she admitted.

She reached into the drawer and brought out her favorite strap-on. Gray slipped into the underwear harness and then slid the dildo into the ring that held it securely in place. She took Savannah's hips and positioned the black silicon dildo ready to enter her. Savannah moaned as it touched her wetness. Gray didn't hold back as she thrust her hips and drove the dildo deep inside Savannah.

Savannah moaned loudly. These were the moans that drove Gray crazy with desire. Savannah audibly enjoyed sex and it was the biggest turn on for Gray.

They had hardly touched yet, and Gray was already close to coming. Savannah had that effect on her.

Before Savannah, Gray had never been able to come without her clit being touched, but with Savannah, it didn't take much to push her over the edge. Savannah flattened her top half to the bed while keeping her ass in the air, changing the angle slightly.

The new angle had the base of the dildo banging Gray's pubic bone with every thrust, the underwear that held it in place was tight against her clit. She felt a huge rush building inside of her. She gripped Savannah's hips tightly enough to bruise as she came so hard she saw stars.

Savannah kept fucking herself back on the dildo enthusiastically for a few more strokes as Gray's fingers reached round to her clitoris before she was coming too with Gray's name on her lips.

Gray pulled out and managed to slide out of the strap on, tossing it aside before pulling Savannah into her arms.

Savannah sighed happily as she rested her head on Gray's shoulder. "We should do that more often."

That drew a surprised laugh from Gray. "What, every day isn't enough for you?"

"I'll never have enough of you."

"Tell that to your painting career. When will you find time to paint?"

"Don't you come at me with your logic."

Gray chuckled. "Fine, fine. We'll spend the rest of our lives in bed while the rest of the world keeps going on around us."

"Now that sounds more like it."

"You're ridiculous."

"You love me."

"I do," Gray agreed, pressing a kiss to Savannah's nose.

Savannah nestled closer into Gray. "We should probably clean up," she murmured.

"Later. I'm not done holding you."

Savannah seemed to have no objection to that.

They cuddled for a while before finally getting up to shower. As Gray leant back against the cold tiles of the shower, Savannah knelt between her legs, her mouth insistently working Gray's clit. Gray felt her clit swelling inside of Savannah's mouth and she felt the familiar rush building again. The water pounded down on both of them. She gripped a handful of Savannah's wet hair pulling her face in tighter as she came hard.

All in all, they were both thoroughly sated when they fell into bed together.

It had been an ordinary day, but to Gray, every day with Savannah was a revelation.

She still loved Amelia. A part of her would always love Amelia, but she held Savannah in a different part of her heart, a part that was no less special or passionate. Amelia was her past. Savannah was her future.

"You know, if you'd told me at the beginning that we would have ended up together, I'd have said you were crazy."

Savannah chuckled. "Me too. I really hated you for a while there. But that was before I got to know you. You, on the other hand, had every reason to be frustrated with me."

Gray shrugged. "I understand your attitude. You didn't want a spy from your father coming and reporting back on you. Once you realized that's not why I was here, you were a lot more cooperative."

Savannah nodded, her gaze far away. Gray could tell that she was thinking back to that awful day, the one when Gray had been shot in the stomach.

"Hey. I told you not to dwell on that." Gray pulled the covers back to reveal a small white scar on her stomach. "See? I'm fine. It's hardly the first scar I've gotten on the job."

"It's the first one you've gotten because of me, though," Savannah said in a small voice.

"And the last," Gray promised. "You're a different person now. And besides, you weren't the one who shot me. Lay the blame where it belongs —on the maniacs who hired kidnappers come after you."

Savannah sighed and shook herself slightly, visibly trying to rid herself of her melancholic thoughts. "You're right. Of course, you're right."

The nightmares had just about stopped, but if they ever returned, Gray would be here to help Savannah through them, just like Savannah was here to help Gray when she heard about losing a client, or a friend in the army getting hurt or killed.

Fortunately, those kinds of things didn't happen often. Her life here with Savannah was peaceful and perfect. They had even talked about adopting children in a couple of years.

"I love you," Gray murmured in Savannah's ear.

"I love you too, Gray."

For so long after Amelia, Gray had tried to guard her heart, but Savannah had just broken through all those boundaries like a hurricane, and Gray couldn't be happier that she had. She hadn't realized just how lonely she had been before

Savannah showed her exactly what she was missing in her life.

It had been a bumpy road to get here, but she had never been happier, and she wouldn't change their journey for the world.

BODYGUARD SERIES

Thank you so much for reading the first book in the bodyguard. If you enjoy hot bodyguards protecting their clients, there is plenty more to come! Check out book 2 here:

mybook.to/Bodyguard2

AFTERWORD

Hey! Thank you so much for reading my book. I am honestly so very grateful to you for your support. I really hope you enjoyed it.

If you enjoyed it, I would love you to join my VIP readers list and be the first to know about freebies, new releases, price drops and special free *hot* short stories featuring the characters from my books.

You can get a FREE copy of Her Boss by joining my VIP readers list : https://BookHip.com/MNVVPBP

Meg has had a crush on her hot older boss the whole time she has worked for her. Could it be that the fantasies aren't just in Meg's head? https://BookHip.com/MNVVPBP

Printed in Great Britain
by Amazon